Massanutten Mansion

by Sandra J. Bost

Copyright © 2006 by Sandra J. Bost

Massanutten Mansion
by Sandra J. Bost

Printed in the United States of America

ISBN 1-59781-968-9

All rights reserved solely by the author. The author guarantees all contents are original and do not infringe upon the legal rights of any other person or work. No part of this book may be reproduced in any form without the permission of the author. The views expressed in this book are not necessarily those of the publisher.

Unless otherwise indicated, Bible quotations are taken from the King James Version of The Liberty Annotated Study Bible. Copyright © 1988 by Liberty University and published by Thomas Nelson Publishers.

www.xulonpress.com

DEDICATION

I would like to dedicate this book to my Lord and Savior Jesus Christ for His glory and my family.

My daughter, Susanna was the inspiration for me to take this step and get my book published. Her husband, Paul, published this book for me. Without their encouragement, this book would not be printed.

My daughter, Sarah, who also encouraged me and proofread it thoroughly for me.

My husband, Ken, who has always believed that I could do this and has prayed for me everyday.

My son, Daniel, who is an encouragement to me.

CHAPTER 1

Dark shadows ran across the ground and thunder rumbled in the distance. The air was thick and oppressive. Jessica Weston slowly approached the darkened church. *Where is everybody? My wedding starts in half an hour. Why is the church so dark?*

When she pushed on the large door, it opened with a loud creak. Inside, she was surprised to see the church was filled with people. The only light in the building came from candles along both walls. In this dim light, she could see a coffin covered with flowers lying at the front.

The rustling of her wedding gown sounded loud in the silence of the room. No one spoke or looked at her as she moved down the aisle towards the altar and the flower draped coffin. She wanted to scream at all those people to get them to respond in some way. Her only thought was to see just who was in that coffin even though she was afraid to know.

A man dressed in minister robes approached from a side door and walked past her without a single look in her direction. Behind him walked another man dressed in a black suit with a white carnation in his lapel. To her, he appeared to be the most handsome man that she had ever seen and she wished she could learn who he was. However, the sad expression on his face was so deep that he looked like someone who had given up all hope of happiness. As if in a trance, he moved to the front and stopped in front of the coffin. While she watched, he smiled and quickly resumed his sad, blank stare.

"What's all this? Who are these people? Why won't anyone answer me?" Jessica yelled out her questions. No one turned toward her or acted as if they heard her. To them she was not there. Silently, she moved forward, closer to the coffin and the two men standing in front of it. She had to know who was in there. As she leaned over the edge, lightning flashed and she saw clearly the face of the person lying there. It was her face.

Horrified, she began to slowly back away from the front of the church. Still, nobody took any notice of her or moved. Her only thoughts were to get out of that place so she could think. Finally, she found the strength to run out the back door in to the ever increasing darkness of the storm. As she reached the sidewalk, the storm with its thunder and lightning broke over her. Rain came in huge drops which soaked her dress as she ran down the road. She did not care but only wanted to put distance between herself and that church building with all those silent people and the horror in the coffin. As she ran, she tripped over a root and fell to the ground. She began to cry. From a distance, she heard a voice calling her name. "Jessica! Jessica! Are you awake? Answer me!"

Sitting up in her bed, Jessica was not sure of what was reality and what was a dream. One thing was sure, the storm that was blowing outside was very real and the room was too dark to be morning. She lay back down and hoped that the voice was only a part of the dream and it was not time to get up. The voice would not stop and seemed to be coming from outside her apartment door.

"Jessica Weston! I know you're in there. Don't you go back to sleep or we'll be late for work. Come on, now, open the door. I look pretty silly yelling at this door. Jessica!"

Jumping out of bed, she realized that it was her friend from work, Norma Jean. They were supposed to go to work together this morning. As she turned on her light, she looked around the room to make sure she was really in her apartment and not in that awful church. She sighed with relief as she saw her old sleep sofa and the few "odds and ends" tables and chairs she had purchased at the thrift store. What did it matter if they did not actually match? She was not able to afford any more than these few pieces of furniture: a sleep sofa, one chair, one table, and a bookshelf made of cinder blocks and boards. This held her real treasures, books and especially the Bible that had belonged to her mother. Her musings were cut short because the knocking at the door grew louder.

"I'm coming, Norma Jean. Hold on."

As she said this, she slowly opened the door to find her friend standing with hands on her hips and tapping her foot. Norma Jean Parker was in her early fifties but still had all the bounce of women half her age. She was only a few inches over five feet tall. Her hair had been jet black but was now peppered with grey which gave her a look of wisdom. Many people would have called her face plain but there was a gentleness in her eyes that made her truly beautiful. She was about the same age that Jessica's mother would have been if she were still alive. Perhaps this was why they had become such good friends. The younger woman needed an older woman to be there for her, listen to her problems, and share her joys. Norma Jean was that person.

"Norma Jean, I'm sorry. I guess I overslept."

"That's okay, honey. If I don't get you going, we'll both be in trouble. Back inside and let's get you dressed. Honestly! What would you do without me?"

Norma Jean only paused a minute to look around before she began to dish out orders. "Go get dressed while I put your sofa back together. What a morning - it is turning out to be! It's raining and sleeting and even some thunder thrown in for a crazy mix. We can grab a cup of coffee and a donut at work before the breakfast crowd comes in. You've got to hurry!"

Jessica hurried into the bathroom to get dressed. That dream was still fresh in her mind. She knew why her dream included a wedding because she had been reading a copy of "Brides" magazine right before she went to bed. Lately, she had been thinking a great deal about marriage and how she was not any closer to finding a husband. No good prospects had come into the deli. What she could not figure out was how a wedding and her funeral had entered into her dream. She decided it must be her subconscious telling her that her changes of getting married were slim at best.

"Face it, Jessica, you're an old maid for sure." She spoke to her image in the mirror. After she had dressed in a blue blouse and grey slacks, she took another long look at herself in the mirror. She felt she was not overly attractive but her thin face with a small nose and light blue eyes was pleasing. She could see her mother's face in her own image. Looking down, she believed that her figure was about right, not too thin but well developed. Her main complaint was that she was much too short at five foot, three to look perfect. After putting on her make-up and brushing her hair, she knew she looked acceptable and went out to join her friend to go to work.

Norma Jean was just closing the sleep sofa as she came out of the bathroom. "My, you do such good work. You were right. I don't know what I would do without you."

"Probably be late for work. That blouse looks good on you. The color brings out the blue in your eyes. Are you expecting anyone special to come into the deli, today?"

"Not really, no one special ever comes into Clyde's Deli. It is just the same old crowd and not one man that I would want to marry."

"Listen, Jess, you've got to stop worrying so much about getting married. I keep telling you the Lord has someone all picked out for you. All you have to do is wait for him."

"Sure, I know that. I just wish the Lord would let me in on His plan."

"Be patient, honey. All in His good time and you'll appreciate the wait. Now if you'd just come with me to church you might meet some fine young men, all good Christians, too."

"I've tried to be patient. It's so much on my mind, I'm beginning to have strange dreams. Let me tell you about the one I was having right before you got here. I was..."

"I hate to interrupt you, girl, but we better get going or we will be late. You know how Clyde hates it when we're late. Tell me every detail as we go. Bundle up! It's cold."

Jessica grabbed her coat off the rack by the door and hurried out with her friend. Norma Jean shrugged her shoulders and closed the door. The two women hustled out into the storm. Jessica related the details of her dream but the older woman barely listened. She was thinking the subject of going to church was being squelched every time she mentioned it but she was not about to give up, not yet.

The walk to the deli was difficult as the wind and rain made them cold. They passed only a few people who were also rushing to work in the freezing rain. Jessica thought of Norma Jean's attempts to get her to church. Years before, she had attended church on a regular basis with her mother and had even walked down the aisle at a revival service. She gave her life to Jesus at that meeting and had really intended to live for Him. For a while after her mother's death, she read her Bible and went to church but she had drifted away until at one point in her life she only attended church services when she had nothing else to do. She felt guilty about not going but soon that wore off and she spent most of her Sunday mornings in bed with a newspaper and a cup of coffee.

They were glad to reach Clyde's Deli where they both worked as waitresses; Jessica for almost two years and Norma Jean for ten years. The smell of fresh-brewed coffee and baking donuts greeted them as they came in the door. The small restaurant had many round tables with red and white tablecloths. Along the back wall was a counter which stretched all the way across the room. Beyond the counter was a small kitchen where Clyde turned out the best donuts and sandwiches in town. Here she had found friendship since moving to Harrisonburg. She missed living in Richmond but it held too many memories.

The cold, rainy day only reminded her more of the day almost two years ago. It was a Saturday and her twenty-fourth birthday. Her mother had decided to work an extra shift at the hospital that day. The overtime money she earned was to buy a birthday dinner for herself and her daughter. Jessica waited at home for her mother's return but she was later than usual. She was so excited about going to a fancy restaurant which they usually could not afford.

However, as it became time for her mother to be returning home, freezing rain began to fall. Jessica was not worried for she knew her mother to a careful and patient driver. When her mother was over an hour late, the telephone rang. A nurse at the hospital told her there had been a terrible accident and her mother had been admitted to the hospital.

When she arrived at the hospital, her mother had come through surgery but was still critical. Jessica remembered her mother, her head bandaged, face swollen, black and blue, yet she had such a peaceful look. For hours she sat by her mother's bed, crying and praying for her mother to regain consciousness and talk to her. However, just before midnight, her mother died.

She remembered little of those next few days; the funeral, burial and good-byes to the one person who was closest to her. Her friends encouraged her to stay and finish college there but her mother had left her only a small amount of money. Most of it went to pay their bills. She decided a change of scenery would help. A friend of her mother's helped her choose a school in Harrisonburg and she moved right away. After finding a job at Clyde's, she began to save her money in hopes of going back to school soon at a college in the area.

"Hey, Jess! Get a move on it, will you! We open up in ten minutes."

Clyde's loud voice coming from the kitchen brought her back to the present. She realized she had been wiping the same spot on the counter for quite a while.

"Sorry, Clyde. I'll get busy now."

By midmorning, the weather had become even worse with snow mixing with the freezing rain and sleet. It was a miserable day in the middle of December. Christmas decorations were everywhere and people crowded into the restaurant to get out of the cold that threatened to dampen even the best Christmas spirit. Coffee and hot chocolate sold better than anything else as shoppers tried to warm themselves before going back into the shivering cold. A man entered and sat down next to the cash register while she waited on a customer who was trying to find the correct change to pay her bill. This had given Jessica a chance to look him over carefully.

It may have been that he was a new face or his expensive clothes which first caught her eye but she was immediately intrigued. He wore a dark tan overcoat over a brown tweed suit which looked expensive to her, not the kind of clothes most of the customers wore to this little deli in the middle of the city. Even though he was sitting, she could see that he was tall, maybe even six foot or better. His dark brown hair was wet from being out in the rain without the benefit of hat or umbrella. She especially liked his face with its strong chin, moustache, and a pair of penetrating dark eyes. The eyes seemed to be his strongest feature as they seemed to be looking right through her. Blushing, she turned away to help her customer. However, she could still feel his stare even though she tried to concentrate on what she was doing.

Her hands were shaking as she turned to get his order. "What would you like, sir?" She asked and prayed that he did not notice that her voice was quivering.

The man did not stop staring into her eyes as he spoke in a very deep voice, "Everything looks good here. It is hard to decide. But I believe, I'll have a chocolate cream donut and coffee, one sugar, no cream. Thank you."

Even while she was getting his order and pouring his coffee, he never took his eyes off her. He was making her nervous and she almost spilled the coffee. She hurried down the counter to get away from the mysterious stranger who kept staring at her. She did have to admit that she thought him to be the most handsome man she had ever seen.

As he was paying his tab, he said, "Thanks, Jessica. You've made my day brighter." With no other words, he walked out the door.

Momentarily shocked, she watched him walk out the door. What had she done to make his day brighter? Who was he? She realized her heart was beating way too fast. With a long sigh, she went back to waiting on the customers. The gloom of the morning seemed to disappear. She thought of the brief encounter with such a handsome man and wished he would come back.

She did not hear Norma Jean come up behind her until she said, "Jessica, who was that guy? Do you know him?"

Blushing a little, Jessica looked away. "Well, no. He's a stranger to me. But he sure is a good looker and probably rich, too. Did you notice his clothes?"

"Now, honey. Don't you go getting dreamy-eyed over a stranger. That can be dangerous. You know nothing about this man. He probably says all that to every waitress."

"Yeah, sure, Norma Jean. You're so right. Excuse me but I'd better wait on those new customers."

Secretly, she wished he would come back. However, she realized that probably would not happen.

CHAPTER 2

Jessica had been busier than usual one day in January, as Norma Jean had called in sick. With her friend absent, she had to wait on all the customers at the counter as well as those at her tables. By ten o'clock, she was ready to quit. Dressed in a black suit and red tie, her mysterious man walked into the deli and took the seat next to the cash register just as he had done weeks earlier. She wanted to run over to him and tell him how wonderful it was to see him again but she had a customer to wait on. He could not make up his mind whether he wanted hot chocolate or coffee. Not soon enough, he finally ordered coffee.

Trying not to look too eager, she walked up to the stranger and said, "What will it be, today?"

He smiled pleasantly and looked straight into her eyes and said, "You sure are busy today. Where's the other lady who works back there with you?"

"Well, she's got the flu or something so I'm here alone for this shift. What can I get you?"

"I believe I'll have one of your freshest chocolate creme donuts and coffee with..."

"One sugar and no cream. Right?"

"You remembered! Do you always remember how each of your customers likes their coffee?"

She wanted to say that it was only his coffee she could remember but it sounded too familiar. Just as she gave him his order, the man at the end of the counter stood up and waved at her. "Hey, Jess! Where's my donut? I don't have all day."

"Go ahead and take care of your other customers. I'm not in a hurry today. In fact, I would like to talk to you for a little while. If that could be arranged?"

She looked at him just in case he was kidding her but his smile looked sincere enough. As she moved down the counter, she almost tripped over a box on the floor. "I take a break in about twenty minutes."

"Hey, Jess, that customer needs you." Clyde had come up behind her while she was talking to her stranger. "Get busy, okay?"

Now she hurried over to help the man at the end of the counter and waited on the few customers still in the deli. Even though she kept busy, she was only thinking about the stranger who wanted to talk to her. Since her mind was not on her job, she spilled coffee, dropped donuts and mixed orders. She was wiping up her latest spill when she saw Clyde coming toward her.

"Okay, Jess, take a break before you lose all my customers."

Clyde was standing over her now drying his hands on a towel. His clothes were covered with flour and jelly as if a batch of donuts had exploded all over him. He was a tall man with broad shoulders and large arms that made him look more like a fighter than a deli cook and owner. His red hair and beard were both flecked with grey hairs and flour as usual. If he had not seemed so angry, she would have laughed. "I'll take care of these customers. Be back in ten minutes! Please try to get yourself back together before the lunch crowd comes in."

Even though he was a little angry at her, she did not care. Now she would be able to go and talk to her stranger. When she glanced over to the cash register, he was gone. Alarmed, she looked around the restaurant and thought he must have grown impatient and left. Then she saw him sitting at a table by the door. Seeing her looking his way, he stood up and waved.

Relieved, she poured two cups of coffee, grabbed two honey-wheat donuts and almost floated over to the table. He kept his dark eyes on her as she came across the room. She wondered whether her hunter green skirt was too short or too tight. It was her best outfit with the ivory sweater but she was uncertain if he would approve of it. There was something about the look he was giving her as if he was sizing her up or trying to make a decision about something. Even though she was intrigued by him and curious about what he wanted to say, she felt uneasy as if there were some danger involved with him. She wished that she could get to the table without tripping or doing something stupid. She finally thought, "I'm being silly. He just wants to be friendly. I guess I've been reading too many of those romance novels lately."

"Hello, Jessica." He greeted her as he stood up and took the tray from her. Placing it on the table, he pulled out a chair and helped her sit down. "I'm sorry I have not been back since I first came here last month. But there was something about you which made me feel good and I just had to come here even if only to see you for a few minutes. I hope you don't think I am being forward by talking to you."

"Oh, no, I didn't think that at all. But you have me at a disadvantage, you know my name and I don't know who you are aside from the fact you don't like cream in your coffee."

"I do beg your pardon. My name is Adrian Daniels. It has taken me a while to get up the courage to ask you a question. Would you consider dining with me tonight at the Wild Boar's Inn?"

"I don't know. You see I really don't know you well enough to go out on a date."

She felt uncomfortable sitting in front of this man whose eyes were gazing steadily at her until she seemed to be hypnotized. The silence lasted for many minutes. After it became uncomfortable, he said, "You're right. I have been too forward. It's just in my line of work, you have to make quick decisions. I suppose asking for a date should not be such a quick decision. Maybe if I tell you something about myself."

"I deal in stocks and bonds. I like to help people increase their earnings and insure their future. I haven't lived in this town very long but I like the area and I hope to stay here. In fact, I have been renovating a house east of here. My hobbies are reading and going for long hikes in the mountains. Also I do travel and see a lot of the world in my business. Does that tell you enough about me? I would like to get to know you better."

"That's not exactly what I meant. It's just a girl has to be careful who she goes out with these days and I..."

"I see what you mean, Jessica. All right. I won't press it for now but I hope you'll give me a raincheck for another time. Perhaps after you get to know me, you'll change your mind."

"Sure, that would be fine. I'm sorry I can't go out with you tonight. I hope you understand?"

"Yes, perfectly. I do need to get back to the office now and you to your customers. It seems your boss is becoming a bit impatient. He's glaring at you from behind the counter."

"Oh, don't worry about him. He only growls like a bear but I've yet to see him pounce on anybody. Thanks for asking me anyway."

"See you tomorrow, Jessica, same time. O.k.?"

As he stood up, he took one of her hands in his, leaned over and kissed it. Just as quickly, he left the deli. She could not believe this was happening to her. Stepping behind the counter, she patted Clyde on the back and began to wipe the counter. Secretly, she hoped he would come back and ask her out again.

True to his word, he was back the next day at the time of her midmorning break. He became one of the best customers of the deli as he came in everyday at the same time. He always had new stories or jokes to tell the waitresses. Even Clyde would come out from the back whenever he came to the restaurant. It was clear everyone liked Adrian Daniels especially Jessica who shared her break with him.

Only Norma Jean was not under his spell and she watched him closely. To her, he appeared to be just too good to be true and that he was trying too hard to get everyone to like him. There was something about him which bothered her but she was not sure what it was. Everyday Jessica was getting more and more interested in this man. Other than what he let all of them see, they did not know much about him. Whenever she tried to tell her doubts to her young friend, Jessica changed the subject or walked away without comment. After three weeks, she decided to pray about it and keep quiet.

One day, Adrian was later arriving than usual. Jessica had a difficult time keeping her mind on her work. When he finally came into the deli, everyone breathed a sigh of relief.

Jessica carried two coffees and a plate of donuts over to their usual table. Pulling out a chair for her, he waited for her to sit down before he said, "Sorry, I'm late, Jessica. I hope you will forgive me."

"Of course, I do. Is everything all right?"

"Oh sure," he said as he sat down next to her at the table. "I just needed to work up a little courage to ask you something."

"You? Work up the courage? Oh, please, that's a laugh! I don't believe I've ever met anyone who makes friends as easily as you do."

"That's true. However, I was not referring to that kind of courage. You see, when I first came into the deli a few weeks ago, I asked you to go out to dinner with me. Since you didn't know me, you turned me down. I hope you feel like you can say yes this time."

"Well, I don't know if..."

"Please don't say no right off! We'll have a wonderful time at the Wild Boars Inn. You said yourself that you had never been there and this is your chance. Wouldn't you like to go?"

"Yes, I would. It is just the place is too expensive for my salary." Jessica hesitated as she weighed her desire to go out with Adrian with a nagging doubt and Norma Jean's warnings about him. After all how much did she know about him? Finally, she decided she needed some excitement in her life. Smiling, she whispered, "All right, I'll go out with you. I've always wanted to eat there."

"Then it's settled. I'll pick you up at your apartment at 7:30. Please be ready on time. I don't like to be kept waiting."

As he was turning towards the door, she realized she had not told him her address. "Wait a minute, Adrian! I haven't told you where I live."

"That's okay. I know already. See you tonight!"

She stood by the table for a few minutes and watched him walk down the street. "That's odd," she thought. "How did he know where I live? I can't recall telling him. Oh, who cares? He is sure a mystery and I love that in him. I'll be dining at an expensive and exclusive restaurant with a rich, handsome, and mysterious man. I can't wait."

Just then Clyde stepped over to the table. "Hey, Jess, did Adrian finally ask you out?"

"He did and I'm going no matter what anyone says. He's taking me to the Wild Boar's Inn for dinner tonight. Isn't it exciting?"

"You bet it is. But, Jess, how much do you really know about this guy? Those rich guys can sometimes take advantage of young women. You be careful. Okay?"

"Sure, I'll be careful. You sound just like a father, Clyde. I appreciate it."

"Hey, don't say that! I'm not old enough to be a father yet. I just don't want to see you get hurt. Let's get back to work, shall we."

The rest of the afternoon seemed to drag on and on as she waited for quitting time at five-thirty. She would have only enough time to run home, take a shower, and get dressed before seven-thirty. Her thoughts centered on what she should wear for her man of mystery. All her dresses seemed so ordinary to wear to such a fancy restaurant but she finally made up her mind on her green party dress with the white lace on the front. It was the most elegant dress she owned but still it was dull in comparison to what she imagined women wore to the Wild Boar's Inn. Anyhow, it was her only solution because she did not have the time or the money to go shopping for a new dress.

All the waitresses teased her or said how envious they were of her going out with Adrian. Clyde must have told her a hundred times to be careful during the afternoon. At five-thirty, she rushed out the door before anyone could even say good-bye. She hurried home still excited yet maybe even a little nervous by the prospect of her date with Adrian. Clyde and Norma Jean had been able to place some large doubts in her mind but she was determined to forget them for the time being. When she arrived at her apartment, she found a large box outside the door with her name on it. The logo on the box was from one of the expensive dress stores at the mall.

"Oh, my! What's this?" She exclaimed as she picked up the box.

"A man left that for you not ten minutes ago. I told him I'd take it and give it to you but he just left it and walked away. He wasn't very friendly, if you ask me. All dressed up in some kind of black uniform and gloves like you see those fancy car drivers wear on the T.V. shows. You know they drive rich people around and all that. But I thought I'd better watch it for you so no one steals it. Aren't you going to open it?"

Jessica was startled by her neighbor's shrill voice and she looked up to see the woman standing next to her. The older woman was wearing a faded housecoat with large butterflies of orange and pink. On her head were the ever present curlers in her grey hair. She had never seen the woman without them on her head and she wondered if they could be permanent fixtures. She was thin with a very skinny face which seemed to always be wearing a scowl. Jessica believed her to be the most nosy woman in the apartment building with a nose to match the part.

Before Jessica could answer, her neighbor began firing questions at her. "You get a raise or something? That sure is a high-priced store that box come from. Go ahead and open it! I'm dying to see what's in it."

Jessica wondered how the woman's husband ever got to say anything with her around. In the calmest voice she could muster, she managed to say, "I'm sure I don't know what it is. I didn't order any dress from the store. I've got to get dressed because I'm going out tonight and I don't have anymore time to chat. Good night!"

She opened her door and went inside, closing the door as quickly as she could before her neighbor had a chance to say another word or follow her. It may have been rather rude but she did not want to open the mystery box in front of her. For a moment, she felt a little guilty about her actions but she justified it by thinking that it was her business. Her neighbor was just too nosy. Anyhow, she decided she would make it up to her by sending her some donuts tomorrow.

Carefully, she opened the box with some effort because her hands were trembling from the excitement of this puzzling carton left at her door. Inside the box was a lovely royal blue and white silk dress outlined in a delicate lace of light blue. As she gently lifted it out and held it up to her body, she saw it was the perfect length and fit for her. She stood in front of the mirror and stared at the beauty of the dress. Just as she was about to put it back in the box, she noticed a small box wrapped in blue paper partially hidden under the tissue paper.

Opening it, she found a string of pearls and a ring with an oval shaped stone of sapphire. On a card inside the small box were the words, "I cannot wait until 7:30. Here are a few small presents that I believe you will enjoy wearing. I guessed at the size so I hope the dress fits and is to your liking. See you soon!" It was simply signed, Adrian.

"To my liking? He must be joking. What girl wouldn't love to wear these! But should I keep them? Oh, what do I do?"

She put the dress over the back of the sofa and the jewelry on the coffee table. Sitting down on the sofa, she thought, "If only my mother were here to advise me. I really shouldn't accept such gifts from a man whom I hardly know. Then again, they are so pretty! It would be perfect to wear them to the restaurant."

She stroked the dress as she argued with herself over the gifts. Two times she almost packed the dress and jewelry back in the box determined to tell Adrian she just could not possibly accept such gifts. Finally, she said to herself, "Why can't I have these gifts? He can surely afford it."

At that point, she glanced at her watch and saw it was all ready six-thirty. Remembering how he said he did not like to be kept waiting, she rushed around her apartment to get ready. This was going to be the best night of her life with her mystery man.

CHAPTER 3

After rushing around the apartment, she was ready in a short time and sat down in front of the window to wait for Adrian. Promptly at seven-thirty, a black limousine drove up in front of the building and parked. A man in a dark suit stepped out of the driver's side and opened the rear door for Adrian who was wearing a black tuxedo and cape. She watched him until he entered the building and then she took one last look in the mirror to check her make-up. Convinced she looked as good as possible, she stood by the door and waited for him to knock. She delayed opening the door until he had knocked twice because she did want to appear to be too eager. Although she had wanted to open the door even before he knocked.

"Good evening, Jessica. You look lovely in that dress. I believe that I guessed the right size and shade for you. That color brings out the beautiful blue in your eyes. Are you ready to go?"

"Your gifts are beautiful not me. How can I ever thank you enough? I just absolutely love this dress and the jewelry. Do we have time for you to come in for a minute? I'll be ready as soon as I get my purse and coat."

"All right but only for a minute." Stepping into the room, he closed the door and leaned back on it as if to keep it closed. She felt his gaze on her as she went into the kitchen to get her purse. It made her nervous for him to be standing and staring at her as though he was appraising her in some way.

"I wasn't sure whether I should accept such expensive gifts from you." She said this to break the silence which had become uncomfortable to her. "I do love the dress but it seems so expensive. How did you know my favorite color was blue?"

"Please don't worry about that," he whispered as he held her hand. "I wanted to give you something to remember this evening and I didn't want you to feel uncomfortable at the restaurant. This dress will make this evening more special to both of us. Besides, I can afford it. Money was meant to be spent if it'll make me happy."

He began to draw her closer to him as he spoke and she thought he was going to kiss her. Embarrassed, she pulled her hand away from him and looked at her watch. "Shouldn't we be leaving for the restaurant now?"

"Of course, let's go, shall we?"

She breathed a sigh of relief and looked away from him as she took her coat off the rack by the door. Taking it from her, he helped her put it on and opened the door. With a slight bow, he ushered her out into the hall and closed the door. He did not even try to take her hand as they walked down the hall and outside to the car. Her heart felt like she had just run a long race and she was surprised that she could not hear it beating. Had it only been her imagination that he had tried to kiss her in the apartment? Had she really wished he had kissed her? Anyhow, she hoped he might get the courage to try again.

As they were leaving, she hoped that everyone in the apartment building had noticed her getting into the limousine with Adrian. She was sure her nosy neighbor had seen because her door was open and someone was peeking out through the crack. If no one saw her leaving, her neighbor would tell them. She was pleased at that prospect.

During the trip to the restaurant, he talked very little but stared out the window. Twice the silence of the ride was interrupted by a call on his cellular phone. She tried to ignore the conversations but the little bit she caught was concerned with oil and options. Bored with this, she thought more about the questions that bothered her. How did he know where she lived? Why was he interested in her? Just who was this man, anyway?

Before she knew it, they were at the restaurant. It was even bigger and grander than even she had imagined a restaurant could be. A valet helped them out of the limousine and opened the door for them. She noticed Adrian hand the man a bill which she was sure was twenty dollars.

Inside they were greeted by a maitre'd dressed in a white dinner jacket and shirt, black trousers, and a red bow tie. He was a rather large man with a red face which reminded her very much of Clyde only fancier. Once again she noticed Adrian give this man a rather large bill after he escorted them to a table by the window.

She tried not to stare at her surroundings as if she were not used to such elegance. Crystal chandeliers hung from the ceiling and the wallpaper seemed to be made of the softest of blue velvet fleurs-de-lis on an ivory background. All of the tables were covered by a light blue cloth and each had a centerpiece of a candle surrounded by pink and red roses. When she sat in her chair, she thought it was the softest cushion of blue and gold. Their table was in a position which gave her a good view of the room. Every table was full with people dressed elegantly and who were obviously quite wealthy. She was glad now that Adrian had given her the dress and she had chosen to wear it. Her party dress certainly would have been out of place here.

The evening was more wonderful that she had imagined. Adrian had ordered for both of them; Caesar salad followed by a large steak for him and a smaller size for her. Never before had she tasted a steak so delicious and she savored every bite of it. The waiter was attentive and stopped by frequently to refill their glasses. Adrian had chosen a red wine but she refused to have anything but iced tea. At first, he made a joke of her choice of beverage but soon became silent as he ate his food.

Adrian simply stared into her eyes and allowed her to do the talking. His contribution to the conversation was to ask her questions about her past. She began to wonder if he thought her boring for doing so much of the talking.

His most pressing questions concerned her mother. She felt somewhat ill at ease with all his inquiries but she believed there was no harm in talking to him.

"So your mother worked as a nurse in North Carolina. What did your father do?"

"I don't really know. You see, my father died when I was two years old. I don't even remember a whole lot about him except he had large and strong arms which I loved to lie in. Mother probably told me more than that but I can't remember what she said."

"Anyhow, Mother went back to nursing to support us because Dad left us very little. She was a live-in nurse for people who wanted to be at home instead of in a hospital. Part of her pay was that we got room and board at the patient's house. When her services were no longer required, we moved to another job. We moved around a lot in North Carolina in those days. She took jobs all over the state."

"When I was ready for school, she took a job at a university hospital in Richmond, Virginia. We lived in a boarding house across town from the hospital. We didn't have a lot of money but we were happy. Some other ladies who lived at the house watched me after school until my mother came home. I had some good friends there. I graduated from high school and worked in a restaurant while I took a few courses at a community college and hoped to attend a university to study nursing later. Even though she had to work so hard, Mother never complained. She always said, 'Don't worry, honey. The Lord will see us through and take care of us. After all, we have each other.' She was a good Christian and took me to church a lot."

"When did your mother die?"

"It was only two years ago. I'll never forget that day. It was a Saturday and the day after my twentieth birthday. We had planned to go to dinner that night to celebrate. But it was raining and she was late and I..."

Jessica looked away from Adrian because she felt the tears coming to her eyes. Crying on her first date with him would not be good. He touched her hand and said, "I'd like to hear about your mother but if it's too painful, then let's change the subject."

"Oh, no, I'm all right. A nurse at the hospital called and told me that my mother had been in an accident and for me to come right away. When I got there, she had just come out of surgery and was in intensive care. It was so hard seeing her all bandaged up with tubes running in and out of her. I prayed to her to recover. It was no use. She passed away a little before midnight."

"For a while, I didn't know what to do. Then a good friend of my mother's suggested I move here and go to school. She gave me letters of recommendation but I haven't used them yet. Perhaps next fall, I'll enroll in the school."

"One part of your story sounds interesting. What about all those families you lived with while your mother worked as a nurse? Do you remember any one in particular?"

"No, not really. Most of them didn't bother with me. I kept pretty much to myself."

"Surely one sticks out in your memory. Maybe a kind old lady or man that did take notice of you or a relative of yours or your mother."

Jessica noticed he was looking at her quite intently now. Why did he care about her mother's former patients? Tension seemed to rest between them now. They both went through the motions of eating but she was not sure if she was enjoying the dinner as much as she had a few moments ago. He became quiet but continued to stare at her. She tried to think and finally she said, "Wait a minute, I remember one patient. He was an uncle or cousin of my mother."

"What was he like?"

"I don't remember a whole lot because I was so young. We stayed with him about a year or so. He was so sick and everyone thought he was going to die. My mother nursed him back to health. While he was recovering, we used to have long talks together. He was so kind to me."

"Do you remember his name?"

"I can't imagine why you want to know his name. Let me think. His name was Thomas something or other. I remember because I always called him by his first name. He wouldn't let me call him uncle or anything like that. His name began with a "g" I think. Oh, what was it?"

She looked away from him as she tried to remember the name of the man who had once been kind to her and her mother. It seemed like a long time before she said, "Now I remember. Thomas Garland. That's it. His name was Thomas Garland and he is a lawyer in Hickory, North Carolina."

At the mention of the name, Adrian looked away. She wondered if she had said something wrong. The silence lasted a moment for he turned around with a smile on his face. "We'd better go now. You've got to be at work and I've got many clients coming early tomorrow."

He quickly paid the check and left a large tip for the waiter. She took a long look around the restaurant and was surprised to see that they were among the last ones to leave. Time had gone by so fast. In a way, she was reluctant to leave because she was sure she would not be back there anytime soon. Back in the car, the trip to her apartment seemed to be too short. Once again her companion did hardly any talking but spent most of the time looking out the window. At her door, she worried if he would repeat his attempt to get close and kiss her. In a way, she secretly wished he would try. However, he simply waited until she opened her door and said good night. She thanked him for a lovely evening. Before leaving, he asked for a date on Saturday and she accepted.

What followed that evening, were weeks of dating and fun with Adrian. He showered her with gifts of jewelry, flowers and even stuffed toys until her apartment took on the appearance of a strange zoo. She had told him how much she had loved stuffed toy animals when she was a girl but her mother could only afford to buy her one very small teddy bear. After three months of all this attention, she felt that she must be falling in love with him even if she had not known him very long.

Each day that he was unable to be with her were hard days. If he was away on business, he had someone deliver a stuffed toy animal, flowers, or candy to the deli for her. Most of the time, he was away on some business deal in either South Africa or Alaska or some remote part of the world. The only way she knew where he had been was the postcards with the postmarks of that place which he sent her. However, he never discussed any of his business dealings with her. If she asked, he dismissed her by saying he was tired of talking business and only wanted to talk about her and what she had been doing while he was gone. For a time, she accepted this but it only made her more curious.

Spring flew by so quickly while she was with Adrian. He had a way of making her feel so wonderfully feminine and for once in her life, important. He told her very little about himself except one day he answered, "Well, there is so little to tell that's interesting. I am thirty-three, not quite over the hill, and am in good health as near as I can tell. Ten years ago, I graduated from the College of William and Mary with a major in business. Not very exciting is it?"

"That tells me something, but I'd like to know everything about you. You seem to know so much about me all ready. One thing you never seem to mention is your family. Tell me something about them, please."

"My family is my business not yours!"

His eyes glared at her as if she had hit a rather sensitive nerve. When he saw the hurt expression on her face, he said, "I'm sorry. I didn't mean to snap at you like that. But you see, I don't like to talk about my family because I...I don't know them. Most of them are not living. To be honest with you, I don't enjoy talking about myself. So let's drop it."

"All right. There is one other thing I wanted to know for it had been bothering me for some time. Just how did you know where I lived that first time you took me out? I didn't tell and neither did any of my co-workers at the deli because I asked them."

At her question, he looked down and said, "I looked it up in the telephone book under your name."

"That's fine. I just wondered, that's all."

The expression on his face told her that he did not plan on saying anymore. She thought, "Now that is odd. The telephone number is still listed under the former occupant of my apartment. There is no way he got my address out of the telephone book. Why is he being so mysterious? Why can't he just tell me the truth like he followed me home or something? Why is he lying to me?"

She could not shake the questions in her mind the rest of the day. In spite of the reservations about his honesty, she still believed she loved him. Perhaps as they got to know each other better, he would be willing to open up to her and be honest. Still there was always a feeling of apprehension as if she were walking into some kind of trouble.

CHAPTER 4

Jessica was so happy when she was with Adrian. Everyday, he was in the diner as she went on her morning break. When he was in town on a Saturday, they went to another restaurant. She kept hoping that he would tell her more about himself but he only wanted to talk about other subjects. Despite all the time they spent together, he was still a man of mystery to her. The trouble was that she was in love with him.

At her apartment, he would come inside for a few moments when he picked her up or brought her home from a date. She knew he lived in an expensive apartment on the other side of town while his house was being finished but he never took her there. When they had a date, he picked her up at the deli or at her apartment. His explanation was that his roommate did not want a woman in their apartment.

Even these little puzzles did not deter her from the fact that she was in love with him. Every day she thought of the time they would spend together and counted the hours and minutes until she saw him. Whatever she was doing, something reminded her of him. If she was shopping, she found herself looking for clothes to please him. She began looking at the men's section of the stores for things he liked and pretended she could buy them for him. At work, she saved the last chocolate cream donut for him when he came in each morning.

For now, he gave her gifts and took her on dates, but he did not say he loved her even though he spent a great amount of time with her. She daydreamed about him saying he loved her and becoming lovers instead of just friends. That moment on their first date when she thought he tried to kiss her had not been repeated. Secretly, she hoped he would try again.

Perhaps their relationship would have continued in this manner until one day in May. Adrian came into the deli at the usual time. Rushing over to the counter, he called out to Clyde who was in the kitchen. "Hey, Clyde, be a good guy and let Jessica have her break now. I really need to talk to her."

Usually Clyde got upset at anyone trying to change his schedule but he was in a good mood and said, "Sure, Adrian. Only ten minutes though. The lunch crowd will be here soon and I'll need her right back behind the counter."

Jessica did not wait for him to change his mind and dashed out to their usual corner table. When they were seated, he looked so serious that she was afraid he had some bad news for her.

"Jessica, over the last few months, we have been together quite a lot. Well, I have really enjoyed those times and I hope they will not end. I have not told you but I am renovating a manor house on an estate just east of town at the base of Massanutten Mountain. It was purchased last year and I wanted it to be a surprise for you. I can't wait to show it to you. I didn't want to take you there until it was finished. The contractor put the finishing touches on the main building just last week. It is my wish to live there after I found someone to share it with me. So you see, I can't wait any longer. Will you consider becoming my wife and living there with me?"

For a moment, Jessica was not sure she had heard him correctly. He had spoken in such a business like manner that she was confused. Was he really proposing?

"Are you asking me to marry you? We've only known each other for a very few months. I just don't know what to say."

"Of course, I want you to marry me. Even though we've known each other for a short period of time, I feel like I know you very well. Every day, I look forward to the time we will spend together. I hated to go on my business trips and leave you here. I love you more than you understand even if I have trouble expressing it to you. You are the right choice for me and I thing you know that."

The words were right and just what she had always dreamed of hearing from a man that she loved but the emotion was not there. It was more if he were negotiating a contract with one of his clients that asking her to be his wife. Was this sincere? Where was the passion that he spoke of? Looking at him, she saw that he was staring at the table and not at her.

Searching for the right words, she said, "I just can't say now. This is so sudden. You hadn't given me a hint about this before..."

"You got to see this is so right for us both. I know I have a problem expressing my thoughts but I have been here for you. I love you and that's all that matters to me. Please say yes."

She hesitated and looked down at the floor. At this point the confusion she was feeling made her want to run from the table. All she managed to say was, "It is sudden. Too sudden...I'm confused."

"Don't be confused, darling. I love you and you love me so why not say yes. You want to, you know. I'd like to set the date on June thirtieth. What do you say?"

"That's so soon! There wouldn't be time to make any arrangements, send out invitations, get..."

"Now, you don't have to worry about all that. The ceremony that I've planned will be private with only a minimum number of witnesses to satisfy the laws of the state so we don't need invitations. Mrs. Simms, my housekeeper, will take care of all that. We can have a big party for our friends when we return from our honeymoon. I just can't wait to do all that traditional stuff."

"The church needs to be reserved ahead of time. Can you do that now?"

"I'm sorry, but under no circumstances will the ceremony be performed in a church. We will stand before a justice of the peace and..."

"But...but I have to be married in a church. You see, I'm a Christian and it is important that I be married in a church."

"No! It is out of the question. We don't need a preacher to marry us. Look, I do love you and I want to marry you. I've got to go now. You don't have to give me an answer now. Think about it a little if you wish. I'm sure you'll see it like I do and say yes. I'll pick you up at your apartment at six for dinner. You can give me your answer then."

He spoke the words in a hurry but before he left, he grabbed her around the waist and lifted her up to him. His lips met hers and caressed them for a long time. When he let her go, she was out of breath and so stunned by his sudden show of passion that she fell back into her chair. Without another word and oblivious to the fact that every eye in the deli was on him, he strolled out the door.

Clyde was the first one to break the silence. He had come out from behind the counter and was standing over Jessica who was still sitting dazed in the chair.

"Hey, Jess, are you all right? What was that all about?" He asked as he sat down across from her.

With great effort she whispered, "I'm all right, Clyde, really I am. I appreciate your concern. It's just that Adrian asked me to marry him."

"Congratulations, Jess! Hey, everybody, that guy finally asked our Jess to marry him! Isn't that great?" He seemed more excited that she was at that moment. All the waitresses crowded around them and she related all the details at least twice. All of them had an opinion of what she should tell Adrian and were not afraid to express it.

One of them asked, "You are going to say yes, aren't you? I sure wouldn't let a rich guy like that pass me by if I had the chance. Not that I'm complaining, mind you, because I'm happy with my man and kids. But you just have to say yes or you'll regret it the rest of you life."

"I'm not so sure. For some reason, he's against a church wedding and I've always dreamed of being married in a church."

"So? My Bill and I were married by a justice of the peace and we're happy," said another waitress.

"This seems awful sudden to me, Jessica. You've got time to think about this, I hope." Norma Jean said as she sat down next to Jessica.

Jessica looked at the older waitress who was her best friend at the restaurant. She felt she trusted Norma Jean because of her concern and that she was a Christian also. She answered, "I'm not getting any younger but that's not the point. It's all happened so quickly. I just want to be sure that's all. If only I could make up my mind. What should I do, Norma Jean?"

"Hey, girls! Let's get back to work!" Clyde yelled across the room. "The lunch crowd will be here any minute."

All the waitresses except Jessica and Norma Jean hurried back to their stations. The two women wanted a few minutes to talk before getting back to work. Norma Jean knew that her friend was confused and needed her advice, but she was beginning to believe that Jessica had already made up her mind to accept and only wanted assurance that it was the correct decision.

"Do you love him, Jess? Does he really love you? If he did he wouldn't have told you this way. He'd then give you all the time to think about it. Not a couple of hours."

"Yes, I love him very much. I can't bear the thought of losing him. He does love me. I know he does. I just wish he'd want a church wedding like I do. But it may not be that important, really."

"Yes it is, honey. It is to you so it should be important to him also. My husband and I were married by a justice of the peace years ago. It wasn't until after we were saved that we knew how important a church wedding is. Why, even with two kids, we did it proper at our church and that made a whole lot of difference to us. Why don't you and Adrian go talk it over with my pastor. Seems funny to me, he can't go into a church once to get married."

"He says he can't wait to marry me. The date he wants is June thirtieth. Anyway, he says he doesn't like churches and I've got to let him know tonight. There's no time to talk to your pastor or anyone else."

"Doesn't that bother you that he's against a church wedding?"

"A little, but..."

"It should bother you a lot. Don't you see, he's rushing you for some other reason. There's all the time in the world to make this kind of decision. This is a forever decision, not what you plan to eat for supper tonight. You're a Christian and you know I'm right. Tell him you need more time. My pastor can talk to you tomorrow."

"No, that won't work. Norma Jean, you see I've just not been going to church like I used to do. When my mother was living, we walked to a little church in Richmond just about every time the doors were open. I even went forward at a revival meeting and I really intended to live for Jesus but that was so long ago. Oh, I went for a while after she died because I knew she would have wanted me to go. Now

I go when I feel like it. So maybe it isn't that important to me either."

"This can't be God's will for you. You're saved, I'm sure of that even though you're fighting against it now. From what you've told me about him and what I've seen, I'm positive that he isn't saved. The Bible says in II Corinthians 6:14, 'be ye not unequally yoked together with unbelievers...' and you can't chance that. If he really loves you, he'll wait and if not you're better off without him. You just don't know him or a lot about him, do you? You don't have enough facts to make such an important decision this quickly."

"All I know is that I love him and don't want to let him out of my life."

Jessica felt close to tears as she got up from the table. She did not understand why Norma Jean, her best friend, was not positive like the others seemed to be. She certainly did not need any more doubts right then.

"All right, Jess. You'll make the right decision. I want you to be happy and I believe you should think this through carefully before making such a big move in your life. I'll be praying for you this afternoon. C'mon, we'd better get back behind the counter before Clyde has a heart attack."

The rest of the day dragged on endlessly for Jessica. What should she do? Here was a handsome and rich man who wanted to marry her. It was as if her life was a fairy tale. She was sure of her love for him. On the other hand, he seemed to be rushing into this marriage. Today was the really the first time he had ever showed such passion for her. Many times he said he loved her but never like he did today. Why was he in such a big hurry to get married? Was a church service so bad? She had to admit that everything Norma Jean had said was right even if she did not like hearing it. How well did she really know him?

Many times she tried praying, "Lord, please tell me what to do. I am so confused. Please tell somehow just what I should do." Yet even as she kept saying that prayer over and over, she felt little comfort and no answer.

Every time she would look at Norma Jean, her friend smiled and put her hands together like she was praying. They did not have time to do anymore talking because of the crowd in the deli, but she knew Norma Jean wanted to give her more advice. All she was able to do was pat her hand as she passed and say "Keep praying, honey. I am."

Finally, just before quitting time, she thought, "Since no one will help me make the decision, I've made up my mind. The others were right, I'd be a fool to let Adrian get away. I can't wait forever for someone to marry. A church wedding isn't necessary and besides, I haven't been to church in months. His love for me will only grow stronger after we're married. After all, God must have allowed him to come into my life so it has to be right. He'll come to know Jesus someday. I just know it. I'm going to be happy again."

Having made this resolve, she felt much better. As she was leaving, she told Norma Jean, "I've made up my mind. I'm going to marry him."

"All right, Jess. You know how I feel about it but it is your decision to make."

"I do appreciate all you said. I know you are only thinking about what is best for me. Adrian is what is best for me and I can't let him go."

"Oh, Jess. I hope and pray it works out for you. Just make sure that you don't forget all your poor friends when you're living in that big mansion, you hear. I do care about you and I'm always here for you."

She gave her young friend a hug and said, "Hey, you better not keep your man waiting. See you tomorrow!"

"Thanks, Norma Jean. You'll always be my special friend. Of course, I won't forget you. I'll be inviting you and the others to my new home real soon. Please tell the others because I'm late as it is."

"I sure will. Don't forget your umbrella! You left it behind the counter, I think. It looks like rain."

Jessica retrieved her umbrella and started to leave. As she was passing the kitchen, she heard her friend praying, "Dear Lord, watch out for Jessica. She is sure running toward trouble, I fear."

She hurried out of the deli before she could hear anymore of the woman's prayer. Her mind was made up and she did not want to go over it all again. At her apartment, she just had enough time to change her clothes before he arrived at six o'clock.

When she still had some doubts, she dismissed them by saying out loud, "It'll all work out. After all, God wants me to be happy" or "I'm sure God can use my life to help Adrian become a Christian after we're married." These thoughts made her feel better as she dressed.

The doorbell rang promptly at six o'clock and she felt a sense of apprehension again. "It's just nerves, that's all," she whispered as she opened the door.

Chapter 5

As Adrian entered, he caught her in his arms and kissed her as if he did not want to let her go. The room seemed warmer to her as if their lips meeting had created a fire. He drew her closer to his body so that she felt his heart beating wildly against her chest. Pulling her lips away, she remained in his arms while he closed the door and led her over to the sofa. Now sitting so close beside him, she was willing to say anything to him if only he would kiss her again like that.

He whispered in her ear, "You are so beautiful. I do love you! Please say you'll marry me. I want you so badly."

"Yes, yes, yes! Of course, I'll marry you. I couldn't live without you."

As she said that, she drew his face back and kissed him as hard and passionately as she knew how. He drew away after only a moment before he pulled her closer once more. She wanted their embrace to last forever. To her this was how it was always going to be between them. She knew at that moment that she had made the right decision because their love was on fire and so right. She did not care about anything else as long as he kept on holding and kissing her as he was doing. "He does love me, he loves me," was all she could think.

All too soon the mood changed as Adrian drew away and stood up. "Wonderful!" He said as he straightened his clothes and hair. "Jessica, you've made me a very happy man. Let's go to the Wild Boar's Inn and celebrate. How soon can you be ready? I was so sure you'd say yes that I made reservations for seven."

The spell was so suddenly broken that she sat on the sofa staring at the man who was so loving and passionate a moment ago but now so businesslike and cold. She felt stunned and hurt at the change in his attitude toward her. Those few moments were so wonderful. How did it change so completely?

"I thought we could stay here and make some plans. Let's order a pizza. We could spend some time alone together."

She shifted her position on the sofa and even patted the empty space beside her. It seemed like the best hint without actually telling him to sit down. She wanted him to be like he had just been, loving and so passionate.

"Celebrate here? You must be joking! As I told you, I've already made reservations for seven. If we don't hurry, we'll be late. So go change your clothes quickly."

He turned away from her and looked out the window. Only then did she notice he was wearing a light blue dinner jacket and black slacks. He had dressed up to get her answer. This man was a bit overconfident about himself. For a moment she almost told him if that was his attitude toward her, he could just forget the whole thing.

As she stood in front of the wardrobe getting down one of her fanciest dresses, she remembered what it was like without him. He was right after all and going to the place of their first date was a more appropriate way to celebrate than sitting in her apartment eating pizza. Looking at her plain green jumper and turtle neck shirt, she understood why he wanted her to change. She decided she would do anything to please Adrian and if changing her clothes to go out with him pleased him, she would do it.

She glanced over at him one more time as she went into the bathroom. His gaze had not changed. He was still looking out the window and pacing the floor.

The look on his face as she came out showed he was pleased at her appearance. He came over to her and hugged her close to him. In a way, she hoped he would change his mind and spend of the rest of the evening with her here. Her heart was racing as her kissed her once more. It was an all too brief embrace.

As he released her, he said, "You look wonderful, sweetheart! All the men at the restaurant will be envious of me when we walk in. I'll love every minute of it since I know you will always be mine. Let's go."

He offered her his arm as they were walking out the door. She was glad he was holding her by the arm because she was not sure if her legs were working properly. Feeling as she did, she thought she could float down to the car. After all, it was not every day that a woman gets a proposal of marriage from such a handsome man as Adrian. She wanted to shout to all the people looking out their windows, as she was sure that they were, that she would soon be Mrs. Adrian Daniels. She knew how jealous they would be.

The ride to the restaurant was subdued. He sat back in the seat next to her and closed his eyes. They did not talk at all. Each time she tried to start a conversation, he answered only in a few words and said nothing else. Soon she decided to give up talking and look out the window. He must be really tired was her only thought. At the restaurant, he will perk up for me.

After being seated at their table, he broke the silence by saying, "Oh, by the way, I'll be going out of town on business next week. Can't be helped. Don't you worry, I'll be back the day before the wedding and-"

"Do you have to go?" Jessica broke in, "Why can't they send someone else? I thought we could spend some time together. We need to make plans. Besides all that, I'll miss you."

"Yes, I have to go because I'm the only one who knows how to handle this account in London. It's not my choice but you've got to go where the boss sends you if you want to keep your job. My vacation time is set for when we will take our honeymoon and I'll need to make money to pay for it. When I get back, we can get our blood tests and such. Then we'll be married and winging our way to sun and fun in Hawaii."

"Oh, all right, I guess if it can't be helped. But when we're in Hawaii, I'll have you all to myself. I was hoping we'd go shopping together for clothes and especially my wedding dress."

"No, no, I hate shopping. In fact, I have my housekeeper buy all my clothes for me. If I don't like what she buys, she takes them back and gets something else. Shopping is not for me. Besides, isn't it considered bad luck for the groom to see the bride's dress before the day of the wedding?"

"Oh come on now, you don't believe that, do you? I just want your opinion, that's all."

"My opinion isn't worth very much when it comes to women's clothes, especially wedding dresses. You are not to worry about picking out a dress. I'll get my housekeeper to pick out two or three dresses and bring them to your apartment tomorrow for you to try on. But if you really wanted to please me, you could wear the dress that I bought you on our first date. Let's just keep it simple. Who needs a wedding dress if you're only standing in front of a justice of the peace?"

"Well, that dress is lovely and I do like it a lot," Jessica conceded, "I've always dreamed of wearing a white wedding dress and carrying a huge bouquet of flowers. But if you want to keep it simple, I guess a special dress isn't necessary. After all wearing the dress I wore on our first date will be romantic. Don't bother your housekeeper about buying any dresses."

"That's my girl! I'm not marrying a dress, I'm marrying a very sensible lady who knows the value of money. Besides, the less money we spend on a dress which you only wear once, the more we can spend on clothes for our honeymoon."

Just as she was about to speak, the waiter approached with the menus. The next several minutes were spent in Adrian ordering two steak dinners for them. While she waited for him to finish talking to the waiter, Jessica was able to think about what had just happened. He had asked her to marry him but there was no excitement. It seemed like they had mutually agreed upon a contract for a business deal and not a marriage.

As they waited for their food to be served, another waiter approached their table and whispered something to Adrian. She was not able to hear what was said but he explained that he had an important telephone call at the desk. He promised he would only be away for a few minutes. However, his few minutes soon lengthened into fifteen minutes and then into a half hour. She was not sure whether she should begin eating as their orders arrived before Adrian returned. Just as she decided to look for the waiter to inquire where Adrian had gone, he returned.

"Sorry, Jessica, but that call was important. I thought I'd never get off. These steaks look delicious, don't they?"

He offered no further explanation of his long absence or the phone call. Jessica waited but he only began to cut up his meat and eat. It seemed to her that he was purposely evasive about it and even looked around as he was eating to avoid making eye contact with her. Just what is he hiding was her first thought.

Finally, she spoke up, "Adrian, I was getting a little bit worried when you did not come back so soon. Don't you think you owe me an explanation?"

Dropping his fork on the plate, he looked straight at her and said, "No, I told you it was an important telephone call for me. You don't need any more explanation than that. You'll have to get used to the fact that I will be getting many such calls and I have no control over how long it takes. My clients are very important to me and I won't cut them off just because you want me back at a certain time. Eat your food before it gets cold."

She was stunned at the reaction to her simple question. He calmly went back to eating and she felt that she should do the same. At that point, the evening was less than perfect and she ate even though she had little appetite. The rest of the time in the restaurant was spent in small talk about their coming trip to Hawaii.

On the way back to her apartment, Adrian reached over to her and pulled her close. He held on to her while he stroked her hair and kissed her on the forehead. Then just as suddenly, he pulled her head up and kissed her until her breath was taken away. When he released her, she had to gasp for air. This was totally confusing to her just after his cold behavior in the restaurant. What kind of man was this? He was cold one minute and hot the next.

Adrian sensed her confusion and said, "Look, Jessica, I'm really sorry about how I treated you in the restaurant. I should not have stayed away on the night that we were celebrating our engagement. The call was a private one between myself and one of my best clients. He was upset about an investment and it took me a while to calm him down. It bothered me that he didn't fully trust me since I've helped him make a lot of money. I was upset but I shouldn't have been so sullen about it. Will you forgive me?"

"Of course, I forgive you. Just give me a little warning before you grab me like that! Okay?"

"If that's what you want but I plan on doing that a lot after we're married. We didn't have dessert or a toast to our engagement, did we? What do you say we stop off at a night club near here and have an engagement toast? We can find a quiet booth and make a few plans together. Would you like to do that? You don't have to be in early, do you?"

"Well, all right. You know I don't drink."

"No problem. We'll just order you a ginger ale or something like that. I'll have a champagne cocktail and we'll talk and celebrate some."

Leaning forward he gave directions to the driver and settled back looking quite pleased with himself. Jessica took his hand and laid her head on his shoulder. They were silent until they reached the small night club on the outskirts of the city. Since it was a weekday evening and early at that, there were few cars in the parking lot. She was nervous at first about going into the bar because it did not seem like the kind of place her mother would have approved. She convinced herself that it would be all right since it was a special occasion and she was not going to drink any alcohol.

Inside, the lights were very dim and it was difficult to see anything. It was a small room with tables and booths, all with candles burning. The bar took up an entire wall to her left and there were plenty of stools for the patrons. She had never seen so many bottles as those on the shelves behind the bar. To the right of the bar, she could see through the doorway into a bigger room. It appeared to be some kind of dance floor.

On all four walls there were mirrors of many shapes and sizes. These served to reflect the light of the candles and gave the room the appearance of being much larger. At the other end from the bar, she noticed a small, raised platform with a stool, microphone and grand piano. She assumed it was used for entertainment although no one was performing at that time.

There were only a handful of people in the room, most of them seated on the bar stools. They only waited a few minutes before a young woman dressed in a very tight and short black dress showed them to a booth away from the bar. She was not happy when Adrian put his arm around the woman's waist and whispered something to her. She did not resist but only giggled and nodded her head. He then slipped her a ten dollar bill as she walked off to the bar.

As he sat down next to her in the booth, she said curtly, "You come here often, Adrian? You seem to know the waitress very well."

He seemed to ignore the tone of displeasure in her voice and answered, "Actually, I do come here quite often. Many of my clients enjoy conducting business here rather than at my office. You get to know the regular waitresses very soon and know which ones give the best service. Debbie has waited on me many times. She's almost like a sister to me. You're not jealous, are you?"

"No, but, well...Yes, I am jealous. You seemed very familiar with her and we are engaged. What did you whisper that was so funny?"

"Hey, cool off now. I haven't gotten used to being engaged. You're right, though, I need to learn proper behavior if I'm to make you happy. Anyhow, what I whispered is a surprise for you. Just wait."

She nodded and realized that being engaged would take some getting used to for both of them. Perhaps she had over reacted to the incident. It was not long before the same waitress returned to the table carrying a tray with two glasses and two pieces of cheesecake. Stuck in each piece of cake was a birthday candle which she lit when she set it on the table.

Smiling, she said, "Congratulations, you two! Adrian is one of my best customers and I'm sure there will be a lot of broken hearts when the news gets around. Enjoy! The boss says it's on the house."

She started to hand the cash back to Adrian but he refused saying she should keep it as a tip. Thanking him, she went back to waiting on some other customers.

"Cheesecake! You remembered. Thank you, Adrian, this was a nice surprise."

"Good, I'm glad you liked it. Now what should we talk about?"

"I'll need to get some clothes and things for our trip. Also we'll need to make arrangements for our blood test and getting the license. There are so many details. How many people can I invite? You know that I'd like to have some of my best friends there. And I..."

"Hey, slow down some. Let's take it one thing at a time. Business has been good so I think we can get you whatever you want. My driver has authority to use my account at a number of stores at the mall. Just give him a call whenever you want to go shopping and he'll take you. We can go tomorrow before I leave and get all the legal things done."

"Sure. Would it be all right if I invite some people from the deli to the ceremony?"

"Of course, go ahead and invite a few people. There isn't a lot of room at the courthouse so it can only be five or so."

"That's perfect, Adrian." She said as she put a piece of the cake in her mouth. Now she was having a few doubts about the ceremony. It sure was not how she had dreamed about her wedding service at all. Again she felt as if he was concluding a business agreement and not the happiest day of their lives. Then again, it is not the ceremony that's important, she concluded, but what comes afterward in a marriage. Now she knew this was what she wanted and needed all her life, a man to love and take care of her. This will work. She managed to smile and reached over and squeezed his hand.

"I wish you didn't have to go away so soon. I'll miss you. When will you be back?"

"And I will miss you the whole time I'm away. I tried to get someone else to go, but no doing. The boss says go and I have to go. I'll be back a couple of days before the wedding."

"All right but we do need to make plans."

"You're right. We do need to discuss the details of the wedding day. I'm not completely moved into the estate as yet. Mr. and Mrs. Simms are an older couple whom I've hired as my driver-butler and housekeeper. They're living there now, just getting the house in order for us. So I thought it would be good for you to move your things into the house the day before the wedding. Then you could spend the night there and get to know them and the house which will soon be yours also. Mr. Simms will bring you to the courthouse for me."

"Where will you be staying that night?"

"I'll be getting back into town that week and I'll call you. Then I'll spend my last night in my apartment. After our wedding, we'll fly to Hawaii for our honeymoon. Don't worry, it will all work out."

"Oh, I'm not worried. It sounds like a good plan to me. I can't wait to see the estate, though. Please tell me about your house, darling."

The rest of the evening was spent in talk about the estate. Adrian described it in detail, the house and grounds plus his plans for furnishing the house. She heard some of his talk but mostly she kept thinking about Hawaii and how happy they were going to be. She imagined them walking on a moonlit beach, romantic dinners and so many hours alone together. The most important part of her dreams was that she was about to become Mrs. Adrian Daniels.

They passed a couple of hours at the club before he took her home. Yet later that night as she was trying to sleep, she could not shake the feeling that something was very, very wrong.

CHAPTER 6

The next week seemed like a dream to Jessica. Each day, Adrian picked her up after work. They had a picnic one day and the next was a walk around the town. The biggest thrill for her was getting the blood tests and then the license. It was true that now their marriage would soon be a reality. All too soon, the week ended and Adrian was leaving town.

It was a cool, rainy day when he stopped in the deli to say goodbye. Clyde offered her the afternoon off and Jessica hoped to go with him to the airport and spend the last moments with him. When he arrived, she would surprise him. She decided to wait in one of the front booths so she could see him before he came into the deli. At noon, Adrian's car pulled into a parking space across the street. As he was getting out of the car, a woman jumped out of another car and ran to meet him. She was a young woman with red hair wearing shorts and tee shirt. Adrian did not seem to be happy to see her and they had a short but excited argument. He pointed across the street and then walked away from her. The woman got back into her car and drove away. Jessica could not help but see that the young woman looked angry.

Adrian sauntered into the deli and sat down in the booth with Jessica opposite her. For a moment she said nothing. Her thoughts were about how handsome he was and how lucky she was to be engaged to him. The silence lasted too long and she knew she would begin to cry if he did not say something quickly.

"Who was that woman, Adrian? I don't believe that I have seen her around here before."

"You mean that young woman who will not leave me alone? She is nobody, really. Her father is one of my biggest clients. I think her name is Beth or Betty. I met her at a party at her father's house and we went out for a couple drinks afterward. She just thinks it was more serious than it was."

"Well, it did look odd to ...."

"Darling, it was nothing so just forget it. I told her that I was coming to meet my fiancé and that she needs to leave me alone. This lunch looks good."

"I knew it was your favorite so I got Clyde to fix it for us. Anyhow, guess what, darling! Clyde has given me the afternoon off so I can go to the airport with you after all. Isn't that wonderful!"

"Not really, Jess. I believe we decided that we'd say our good-byes here and not at the airport. Let's just stick to our original plans."

"But, why can't I go with you? Mr. Simms could drive me back to town. I want to spend every last minute with you and wave to you as your plane takes off. Please say, yes. Clyde is giving us the afternoon."

"I'm glad Clyde is so generous. It is just not possible. I hate to hang around the airport. You'll get bored waiting."

"How can I be bored when I'm with you? It'll be fun."

"No, darling, you don't know what it is like. Besides, I don't want to be embarrassed by a teary scene in public. You'll be crying the whole time. See what I mean? You're already sniffling."

"I'm sorry, Adrian. I'll stay here. You're right, I know I'll cry but I'm going to miss you so very much. Do you have to go?"

"As I'll miss you, darling. But, yes, I have to go if I want to keep my job. It's only a couple of weeks and I'll be back before you know it."

Despite the lunch crowd who tried not to stare, Adrian pulled her close and kissed her. She could feel hot tears welling in her eyes but she fought them back. She did not want him to see her crying. Pulling back, she turned her head and wiped her eyes dry.

With a smile, she said, "Of course, I'll be counting the days, honey, until our big day. You have a good trip. Your lunch is getting cold. Hadn't you better eat it?"

"I'm afraid I'm not too hungry now. I'll get something on the plane. Good-bye, darling!"

He leaned over and kissed her. Without another word, Adrian left the deli. He paused at the door of his car and waved. Just as quickly, he got in the car and it pulled away from the curb. She watched until the car turned the corner and she could no longer see it.

"Are you all right, Hon?"

Jessica was startled by Norma Jean's voice so close to her. She had been so intent on watching Adrian leave that she did not notice her friend standing by her. Her throat felt too constricted to allow her to speak and she only nodded her head. If she spoke she knew that she would break down into tears.

"You can't fool me, young lady. I can see that you're not all right. Did y'all have an argument or something? Why aren't you going to the airport to see him off?"

Swallowing hard, Jessica felt control of her voice returning. "He didn't want me to go there. He said he didn't like teary good-byes in public. I guess he was right. I sure would have cried."

"Like that many people would see or even care! He's got some other reason why he doesn't want you to go there. I am sure of that. But what could it be?"

"Now Norma Jean!"

"Don't now me. I still think you both are rushing this whole marriage. You should give yourselves some time, get to know each other..."

"You're all wrong about him. He loves me. He does. I know it! You just don't like him, that's all."

"Now, Jess. Let's sit down and have a quick coffee. I'll get some for both of us."

Jessica nodded and sat back down at the table where she had just moments ago sat with Adrian. She patted the seat where he had been sitting and wondered again why he was so against her going to the airport. Was her friend right that he had some secret reason for her not going? Norma Jean was gone for a moment when she returned with steaming hot coffee and freshly baked blueberry muffins.

"These just came out of the oven. Clyde said we could try them. He's testing out a new recipe. We're his guinea pigs, I reckon, but they sure smell good."

Neither of the women spoke for several minutes but ate their muffins and sipped the steaming cups of coffee. Her friend waited while the younger woman got control of her emotions. The lunch time crowd left and the deli was empty except for the waitresses. Even Clyde poked his head out of the kitchen to check on his young employee. Despite his usual gruffness, he had a genuine concern for the waitresses in his deli.

After a while the hot brew and silence had its desired effect and Jessica looked at her friend and smiled, "Well, now, I best get back to work."

"Jess, Clyde said you had the afternoon off. I'm sure he'd still let you - no matter. Maybe some time alone is what you need."

"No, I don't think so. It is better to be busy and besides I can use the money for Adrian's wedding gift. He is going to love what I got for him. It's a dark green velvet smoking jacket with his initials on it. I've had it in lay-a-way for a couple of months now. Just a few more dollars and I can get it out."

"My goodness that must have been expensive. How did you afford..."

"It was not so bad. Actually it had been marked down a couple of times. Since I am buying it there, they'll put the initials on for free. He'll just love it. I can see him wearing it after dinner while we cuddle in front of a fire. It's so romantic."

"That sounds wonderful, hon. Do you have plans for tomorrow?"

"Oh, yes. Mr. Simms is going to pick me up at my apartment and drive me to the mall. Adrian wants me to pick out some new clothes for our honeymoon trip."

"That's good. Maybe you can come over to my house after you get back and show me all you buy. I really don't want you to be alone too much. Anyhow after you get married, I won't see you as often. We need to spend some time together now. Just walk over after your trip to the mall is over."

"Sounds like a good plan to me. It's a date. We better get back to work. Clyde is looking this way again."

True to his word, the next morning, Mr. Simms arrived at her apartment at nine o'clock. When she opened the door, he stood with his hat in his hand. For the first time, she noticed this usually quiet man who had always been sitting behind the wheel of Adrian's car. He was not much taller than five foot eight and he was extremely thin. His hair was gray but had begun to recede from his forehead and the few hairs he had were brushed across the bald spot. It was not a very effective job but it did cover up some of his head. His black uniform was neat and everything was in place and tidy. His eyes were large but he held them only halfway open as if he did not want to look fully at her. His nose was thin and bony and he pinched his face together as if he was smelling a bad odor. She did not like her first impression of this man for he did not seem to like her.

"Good morning, Miss Weston," he said in a high pitched voice. "I'm here to pick you up for a shopping trip per Mr. Adrian's orders. Mrs. Simms, my wife, is waiting for us down in the car. Are you ready to go?"

"Yes, I am. Just let me grab my purse. I didn't know your wife was coming along too."

"I hope you don't mind, Miss, but Mrs. Simms thought she could help you pick out clothes that Mr. Daniels would approve. She does know him better than you do, almost like his own mother. Besides she doesn't get many chances to come to town these days."

"That's fine, Mr. Simms. I do need some help after all."

She nodded as she closed her door. It was clear they did not think she was capable of choosing appropriate clothes. She would show them how well she knew her future husband. Anyhow she had no choice since the other woman was already in the car and to refuse would be rude. As she followed the man to the car, she wondered what his wife was like. Could she be any worse than him?

The chauffeur stood at the curb and held the door of the car open for her. She hesitated for a moment to get herself ready to meet Adrian's housekeeper. Inside the car was a woman who was as different from husband as two people could be. She was older looking with gray hair that was drawn back in a bun at the back of her head. Even though she was sitting, it was obvious that she was not only taller than her husband but heavier as well. The old nursery rhyme of "Jack Sprat and his wife" came to her mind almost instantly. It was a wonder that she did not laugh out loud. She dared not for the woman in front of her had a hard face with many wrinkles which showed she was a formidable person not to be trifled with by anyone. Her dark brown eyes were almost black and she stared at the young woman as if she was meeting a challenge. She was dressed in a plain navy blue dress with no frills except for a white collar. Her look of disgust turned quickly to a smile even though it did not seem too sincere or friendly.

"How do you do, Miss Weston. Mr. Daniels has told me all about you. He was correct, you are a beauty. Please get in, my dear, so we can get on with our shopping. I do love to shop. Don't you?"

Jessica entered the car and sat down next to the older woman. "It is very nice to finally meet you, Mrs. Simms."

"Yes, now that we've dispensed with the introductions, let's get going. I've decided we shall go to the mall to pick out your clothes. Mr. Daniels asked me to make the final decision on any purchases. That way, we will be sure to please him. You may go now, Mr. Simms."

Obediently, the driver pulled away from the curb. On the way to the mall, the older woman asked so many questions about Jessica's past that she began to sense that she was on trial. It was a great relief when they arrived at the mall.

The rest of the morning was spent in almost every store in the mall. Each time that Jessica picked out an article of clothing, the older woman disagreed with it. At first, she had decided not to let Adrian's housekeeper bully her into making decisions. It did not take long for her to realize that Mrs. Simms was a woman who would not concede any fight. Anyhow the clothes that were selected were fashionable and did look good on her even if they were not her first choice. It was easier to agree and end the exhausting shopping trip.

After closing her apartment door behind Mr. Simms who had brought the packages up to her apartment, Jessica collapsed on the sofa. Somehow she would have to find a way to get along with that couple. Her only hope was that as

Mrs. Daniels, she would be in charge of the household and they must listen to her. With that thought she changed her clothes and called Norma Jean to see if she was home. Being with her friend was a relief after being with that couple.

    The next weeks went by slowly for Jessica. Each day she went to work and spent her evening at her apartment or Norma Jean's house. She packed her few belongings in boxes from the grocery store. Each box was carefully labeled and stacked by the door. In between packing and work, she dreamed of her wedding day. She just knew that her life with him would be a dream come true.

Chapter 7

The day before her wedding had finally arrived. Jessica spent the morning cleaning her apartment for the last time. After all she did not want to leave this little place in worse shape than when she arrived. She was a little sad as she thought, this is the last time I dust my table or the last time I wipe off my kitchen counter. All around her were boxes packed with her clothes and treasures. Mr. Simms was to come later that day and move all the boxes to her new home. The furniture was staying for the next tenant. With a sigh she walked around the room and sat down to wait for Adrian.

She did not have long to wait, for almost as soon as she sat down, the doorbell rang. Rushing to the door, she flung it open, hoping to see Adrian standing there. Instead, she was disappointed to see it was only Mr. Simms with his hat in his hand and looking most disagreeable.

"Ready to go, Miss Weston?" The little man spoke in a voice barely louder than a whisper. "The car is waiting. I'll come back later for theses boxes."

"Sure. I'm ready. Where's Adrian? I thought he was coming to pick me up."

"Mr. Daniels is waiting for you in the car, Miss. If you'll show me where your suitcases are, I'll fetch them and we'll be on our way."

She pointed to the two suitcases by the couch and the driver carried them out into the hall. She then locked the door for the last time and gave the key to Mr. Simms. What did it matter if Adrian did not come to the door? He was waiting for her in the car. Maybe he had received an important call on his telephone and was talking to a client. Anyhow this was no time to show her disappointment.

As she reached the landing on the stairs, she looked out the window. A woman was hurrying away from Adrian's car. To her shock, she looked like the same woman who had spoken to Adrian outside the deli. Why was this woman following her fiancé? Perhaps it was not as innocent as Adrian explained. After all, he had also been quite friendly with the waitress at that bar he had taken her to on the night of their engagement.

She hesitated until the woman was out of sight before going down the last flight of stairs and out the door. By that time, Mr. Simms had put her suitcases in the trunk and was holding the back door of the car open for her. Adrian was inside and he seemed a bit flustered. His hair was messy and he was somewhat in a hurry to comb it.

"Oh hello, darling. You kind of caught me in a bad shape here. Simms had picked me up straight from the airport. I didn't want to be late picking you up. So I sent him on up while I finished tidying myself up. But you both came back a little soon so I..."

"All right, Adrian. But there is one question that I need to ask you. Who was that woman I saw walking away from the car as I was coming out? She looked like that client's daughter who was bothering you at the deli the other day."

"Oh, that woman. No, she just wanted directions to some store that I have never heard of. Now that you mention it, she does look like her but it wasn't her. Did you think I was making love to someone in the car while I was waiting for you to come down? A slightly absurd thought, don't you think?"

"Of course, I wouldn't think such a thing. It just seemed odd that she should show up here. If she wasn't the woman I thought then there's no problem, of course."

Still she hesitated getting into the car. His explanation did make sense for she had been asked directions many times on the street as she walked to work. However, the woman still looked familiar. He was right, he would not bring a woman right to her doorstep. Tomorrow, he would be her husband so she could then relax.

"Hello, Jessica. Are you going to get into the car or not?"

"Oh, sorry, darling." She decided to put her doubts aside as just a mistake on her part. After all, she had only a quick glimpse. "I guess I was daydreaming."

Getting into the car, she moved over next to Adrian. Before Mr. Simms could get into the car, Adrian pulled her closer to him. Their lips met in a long and beautiful embrace. So engrossed was she in his kisses that neither one of them noticed that the car had moved away from the curb. She wanted this moment to last forever. Here was her happiness and she asked herself how she could possibly doubt his love for her.

After a while he let her go and looked into her eyes and smiled. "You are so beautiful, darling. You just don't know how much I've missed you. We'll be at our new home in a few moments."

She leaned over and rested her head on his chest as they both looked out the window. Neither one spoke as they watched the scenery pass by. Once she started to say something but her fiancé, motioned her to be silent and she was content to sit beside him.

Today, the Shenandoah Valley seemed especially beautiful in the bright, warm sunshine. In the fields and pastures, she could see the cows and horses contentedly grazing. The Massanutten Mountain rose taller in front of them and shimmered in its large green silence. Running away to the north as far as she could see, the mountain cut through the valley. She wondered at its summer splendor and how it was so affecting her now. Ever since she had moved to Harrisonburg, she looked at that mountain to the east but it was always just there. Now it was the most perfect sight to her because right next to that huge mountain was her new home that she would share with the most wonderful man sitting next to her. This was her paradise and they were almost there.

Soon they turned off the main road onto the gravel road, she could hardly contain her excitement at finally seeing her new home. The road twisted back and forth between the trees, narrowing into a one lane road. Just as Jessica thought the road would never end, they crossed a small bridge, took a sharp turn and came out in front of the house.

There was a large front lawn with the greenest grass she had ever seen. It seemed to invite her to get out and run barefoot through it. She promised herself when given the opportunity that was exactly what she would do, and often. The car pulled around a circular driveway and stopped in front of the house.

As Adrian helped her out of the car, they both stood and looked at the house. She gazed in awe at such at the sheer size of the house set back in the woods and wondered just how it was built here. The trees did not seem to be disturbed at all. It was a Tudor style house of red brick and white board with a main section and one wing. Above the entrance the house rose into a round tower with one extra story above the main section. Otherwise the house had two stories and many windows that stared down at them. She imagined the number of rooms this place must have inside. Whoever had built this house had an imagination and favored the Medieval period of time. Just looking at the house, one might imagine themselves to have stepped back in time and were on a visit to a royal lord or lady.

While she continued to look at the house, Adrian grasped her hand and said, "Isn't it wonderful? Takes your breath away, doesn't it?"

"Yes, darling. It is magnificent. I love it!"

"I knew you would. Coming here is always a pleasure for me as it will be for you. The peace and quiet here is so refreshing. The work is not quite finished on it. Some of the rooms still need some work. I am expecting to inherit some money soon so I can finish it and make this our dream house. We are going to be so happy here, just you and me."

Taking her hand, he led her up to the front door. It was a double door made out of very dark wood and studded with heavy black metal grates. The door knocker was a face of a lion and the handles were large rings in black metal.

As they reached the top of the steps, the door was opened slowly by Mrs. Simms. She looked just as stern as she had remembered her. Now she was dressed in a navy dress with a clean white apron. Her hair was pulled back into a white hair net. She did not look very pleased to see them and only said "Welcome home, Mr. Daniels. Hello, Miss Weston." She stepped aside so they could enter.

The foyer took her breath away as she looked up into the tower above her. It reached up to the cone-shaped roof above them and was filled with windows that flooded light over them. A metal staircase circled around and up to various landings at each story. At the top was a small balcony. On the walls were hung some tapestries depicting scenes from the history of the valley. At the side was an old seat with a large mirror on the back and large coat rack on either side of it. It was made of dark mahogany and was even taller than Adrian by an inch or so. She noticed two doors besides the front entrance which led into the two sections of the house.

"Isn't this great, darling!" Adrian broke the silence. "I plan to get some swords and axes and things like that to put on the walls just above the tapestries. Maybe a suit of armor to stand guard opposite the coat racks. What do you think? It will look like my castle then."

"Sounds wonderful, Adrian. But couldn't we put more peaceful things on the walls that will be more inviting to our guests?"

"Oh, I don't know. We'll see. Now let's see the rest of the house, shall we?"

Mrs. Simms spoke up at that moment, "Excuse me, Mr. Daniels, but your lunch is ready and it will get cold if we do that now. Perhaps you could show her the house after you've had your lunch."

Jessica was a bit shocked at the tone of voice of the housekeeper. It sounded more like a mother speaking to her grown child than a servant to her employer. However, Adrian did not seem to notice but only said, "Of course, Mrs. Simms, you are right and we are hungry. We have all afternoon to look at the house. It is just that I am so excited to show this place off to my soon to be wife."

They followed Mrs. Simms through the door on the opposite wall of the tower. At once, they were in the wing of the house and walking down a long hallway which ran the length of the wing. The housekeeper opened the second door to the right and waited for them to go in.

Jessica was amazed as she entered the spacious dining room. The first thing she noticed was the long dark table which occupied most of the room. Along the inside wall was a large sideboard with towels and napkins on top. Next to this were two dark wood china cabinets but with very few dishes showing in the glass front. Along the opposite side of the room were two bay windows complete with seats and bordered by dark blue drapes. Through the windows she caught a glimpse of the woods on the side of the house.

Adrian had pulled out one of the twelve chairs at the table and was waiting for her to sit down. She hurried and sat in the proffered chair. The table was made of the same dark wood as the sideboard and china cabinets. Many small lights flickered in the well polished surface reflecting from the crystal prisms hanging from the chandelier in the center of the ceiling. Jessica thought that Mrs. Simms might not be friendly but she was sure a good housekeeper to get that shine on the table.

"What a good meal, Mrs. Simms. Here now, love, are you going to stare at the furnishings or eat?"

Adrian's words snapped her out of her musings and amazement at the room. "I'm sorry, darling. It's just that this room is so impressive. It's beautiful. But you're right this is a lovely lunch."

She looked for the first time at the plate in front of her. The housekeeper had placed a green salad and some rolls on the table for each of them. She had not seen such a well organized salad except at a restaurant for there must have been at least a dozen different vegetables in it. The rolls looked fresh baked and steaming hot.

"You are right, Adrian. I didn't know just how hungry I was until I saw this. This is really delicious."

She turned to thank the housekeeper but saw that she was not in the room. That woman is just like a cat, Jessica thought, for I didn't hear her leave.

"Where is Mrs. Simms, darling? I wanted to tell how good this lunch is."

"You can tell her later. She went into the kitchen. I asked her to leave us alone for we have a lot of things to talk about. When we finish eating, I can give you a quick tour of the house. What do you think of this room? I noticed you looking around."

"It is the most amazing and lovely dining room ever, darling. The furnishings are wonderful. But I did notice that there were few dishes in the cabinets."

"There's a very simple explanation for that, my dear, and I do believe you'll like it. I had Mrs. Simms get me enough dishes for my own simple needs. I thought you'd want to pick out your own dishes. We can do that after we return from our honeymoon. How's that?"

"Oh, thank you, darling. That was very thoughtful. We can go together and find some wonderful..."

"No, no, Jessica, I told you that I hate shopping of any kind. I'm no judge of plates, cups and such. You'd soon wish that I wasn't along. I think Mrs. Simms is a better companion on such a trip than me."

"All right, if that is how you want it."

"It is the best way. Anyhow, enough of that! Would you like to see the rest of the house? Are you finished eating?"

"I sure do. Just let me help Mrs. Simms clear off the table."

"You will do nothing of the kind! That is her job so let's allow her to do it."

Adrian stood up and pulled her chair back from the table. As they were leaving, he pulled a bell rope hanging next to the door. She could not hear it ring but was sure it alerted the housekeeper wherever she happened to be. She was sure that she would get used to having servants some time. Anyhow she now only wanted to enjoy looking over her new home and spending time with Adrian.

Crossing the hall, they went through another door into a very short hall with no windows. Adrian only paused long enough to say, "This is a short hallway linking the two wings. I believe it was put here so you wouldn't have to go through the tower room all the time. It is quite convenient for all of us. Let's look at the main wing first."

For two hours, Jessica and Adrian looked into rooms in the main section of the house. The living room was also decorated in early American with dark wood furniture. She gasped as she saw the large sofa and three wing chairs made of green and gold fabric. There were three windows on the front of the room facing the driveway and each one had gold drapes. The dark tables were spread around the room and still the room seemed empty. The green carpet was soft and not been walked on very much.

The only other room on the first floor that had been furnished was the study off the living room. In it were only a desk, two chairs and a filing cabinet. These pieces did not seem to fit with the rest of the house as they appeared to be old and worn. Adrian explained that these pieces of furniture belonged to his father and he felt he should hang on to them.

The other rooms on the first floor were not finished as yet. Adrian assured her that she would have fun decorating each one herself. There were five more rooms including a bathroom on the first floor.

Going to the second floor, Jessica was led to the room at the end of a long hallway carpeted in a rich blue color. This room was right next to the tower at the front of the house. Inside was a large canopied bed with blue and gray bedspread and drapes. The chest of drawers and bureau were of light cherry wood. Off to the right of the bed was a door to a large walk-in closet where she could see her suitcases had all ready been placed. There were quite a few suits hanging there but with a lot more space available.

A door to the right of the closet led into the master bathroom which was large and decorated in blue and aquamarine shades. On the wallpaper were pictures of sea shell and flowers. The fixtures were all in a bright white that resembled marble with gold plated handles. The shower was enclosed by glass and was large enough for two or three people to fit into it. A bathtub with a whirlpool attachment was on the right and the two sinks were on the left of the shower. This was the most luxurious bathroom that she had ever seen. Another door led them out into the hall again.

"Well, darling, what do you think of your new house?"

"It's beautiful, Adrian. Can we look at the rest of the rooms now?"

"Well, you can get Mrs. Simms to show you the kitchen later if you like. That and the pantry are the only rooms left that are finished. The rest of the rooms on this floor are not finished yet. There is another bathroom at the other end of the hall and four more bedrooms. You are welcome to look into them whenever your like. The second floor of the wing is the servant's rooms and only the Simms' is finished. If they ask you to come over there, you may but I would like to respect their privacy just now."

"That's fine, darling. I'll look around more later."

"Good. I must go back to the office and tidy up before I go away for two weeks."

"I thought we'd spend the afternoon together and ..."

"I'm sorry. I can't afford to take the time off right now. You do not want me to have to come back in the middle of our honeymoon, do you?"

"Of course not but ..."

"Good. Then I better attend to those last minute things. Just think, at this time tomorrow, we will be on the plane to Hawaii for two weeks, just the two of us. Are you happy?"

"Yes, I'm the happiest woman in the world right now. I'm sure of that."

"Walk me to the front door. Remember that it will only be a few hours before we are married and I can love you as you need to be loved."

Adrian took her hand and led her down the stairs to the tower room. Before he went out the door, he grabbed her and pulled her close to him. His kiss was very passionate and she wanted to stay in his arms for a long time. However, it was brief and he went out the door. She watched him as he got into his car and drove away.

Just as she was turning around, she noticed that Mrs. Simms was standing in the other doorway. She could not help noticing a look of disgust on the older woman's face. How long she had been standing there, Jessica did not know. The silence was awkward until the housekeeper spoke.

"Dinner will be at six o'clock sharp in the dining room. Until then, you can look around the place. If you need me, I'll be in the kitchen. Mr. Simms went to get your things from town. Will you be needing anything now?"

"No, thank you, Mrs. Simms. I believe I will walk around the outside of the house now."

She went out the door without looking back. She stood on the porch for a few moments trying to get her feelings back in order. That woman was certainly rather spooky and disagreeable. But then, what did it matter? Soon she would become Mrs. Adrian Daniels and then she would be happy.

Walking around the side of the house, she went into the courtyard between the main section of the house and the north wing. In the middle was a fountain in the shape of a running deer, water gushed out of its mouth and cascaded down into a small pool. She sat there for a few moments, dipping her hand into the cool water while she studied the house from the back. There was a screened porch attached to the wing near the kitchen. Inside, she could see chairs and divans made out of white wicker with small white plastic tables set between them. Many of the windows on that side of the house were shuttered as if the rooms were not in use. The only window that showed any light was the kitchen and she saw Mrs. Simms busily working on dinner.

"I guess Adrian didn't have any use for those rooms. When we get back from our honeymoon, I'll get busy and fix them up. It will be fun to plan that together."

Turning her attention away from the house, she strolled out into the field at the back. Not thirty feet away sat a white gazebo with more white wicker furniture surrounded by a flower garden filled with roses of all colors. As she stepped inside, she saw that it had not been cleaned in a while. Leaves laid on the floor and the furniture was in need of dusting. After wiping off one of the chairs, she sat down and looked up at the mountain towering so near to her. A breeze suddenly blew through the gazebo and the air was filled with the tinkling music of wind chimes.

"I'm going to love to spend time out here. This could be may own private place when I want to read or think. I'm sure that Mrs. Simms doesn't come out here so I can surely get away from her at times. Adrian will love it here. Maybe this can be a romantic spot for us!"

She thought of Adrian and herself sharing love in the cool of the evening in her little gazebo. No one else would be allowed to come here. It would be their spot to get away from the world together.

She did not realize just how long she had been sitting out there until she noticed the lengthening shadows and a voice calling her name.

Aloud she said, "That must be Mrs. Simms looking for me. Oh my, I am late for dinner. She'll be in her own little stew, I'm sure. Well, little gazebo, I'll be back soon to clean you out and sit here in peace. Next time I come, I shall be a radiant bride!"

Stepping out of the gazebo, she walked toward the house at a more relaxed pace.

Chapter 8

After supper, the remainder of the evening passed much too slowly for Jessica. She had hoped to get better acquainted with the Simms'. However, they had asked if she needed anything and when she said she did not, they went to their rooms. For a while, she tried reading and then watching a couple of programs on television but nothing seemed to interest her. Her only hope was to wait for Adrian's call in her room.

At exactly ten o'clock, the telephone rang and she grabbed it before the first ring had finished. Stammering and somewhat breathless, she was able to say, "Hello. Adrian, is it you?"

The voice spoke in a hoarse whisper, "Jessica? What are you doing answering the phone? Where is Mrs. Simms?"

"Sorry, Adrian, but I just knew it would be you and I'm all alone in this big house. They went to their rooms. I just wanted to talk to you."

"That's all right, honey, I was just expecting Mrs. Simms to pick up that's all. From now on, please, let her answer the phone. It is part of her job and it keeps us from being bothered by a lot of unimportant calls."

"Okay, I will try to remember that. I am really bored. Can you come over even just for a little while? I do so want to be with you and tomorrow seems so far away. Please!"

"Now, Jess, you know we agreed to get a good night's sleep tonight. If I come over now, we'd be up to all hours of the night and be too tired for our big day tomorrow. Besides I may not be able to control myself with you tonight."

"But I miss you and..."

"Just for tonight and then we'll be together every night. Please be patient, darling. It's not easy for me to be here alone knowing you are only a few miles away and all I want is to be with you and love you. We have to wait."

"You're right, of course."

"Good. Now go to sleep and dream of us together in Hawaii tomorrow night."

"Oh, I will, Adrian, and I can't wait. Do you know how much I love you?"

"Yes, I do and I love you. Good night, darling."

Just after she had hung up the receiver, she remembered a question she had been meaning to ask him. Picking up the receiver to call him back, she realized that Mrs. Simms was on the line with Adrian. Had she been listening to their conversation? Even though she knew that she should hang up, she could not resist listening.

Adrian said, "Is everything going according to plan? Just make sure that you answer the phone from now on!"

"Don't worry, Adrian. We've got it all under control. It will work. It must work. Now get some rest and we'll see you in the morning."

"Good night!"

She waited a few moments before she hung up so that neither one would hear the click and know that she had been listening to their conversation. Now she was confused by what she had heard. What plan? Just what were they talking about and did it involve her in some way? Perhaps they were planning a surprise for her in the morning. That had to be it. What else could it be? She immediately prepared to go to bed because there was not anything else to do. At least she thought that if she went to sleep, the morning would come quickly. Sleep became elusive. She tried to pray, but did not feel comfortable in asking God for His blessing. Was she having second thoughts? Hoping that the fresh night air might help her go to sleep, she opened a window over her bed. As she wished for the morning to come, she fell into a troubled sleep.

The next day dawned bright and sunny with a fresh breeze blowing through the open window. Jessica sat up startled for she did not recognize her surroundings. Her first thoughts were, "Where am I and what time is it?". Then she recalled that she was in her new home and it was finally her wedding day. Jumping out of the bed, she began to get ready for the big day.

"Nothing short of the end of the world will spoil this day for me! This is the first day of my life with Adrian." She spoke these words to her own image in the mirror.

Just then there was a knock on the door. "Are you up, Miss? We had best be hurrying if we're to get to the wedding on time. Breakfast is in thirty minutes."

"Thank you, Mrs. Simms. I'll be ready soon. What's for breakfast?"

When the woman did not answer, she realized she had left. Jessica speculated a moment on how a woman of her size could move so quickly and silently. It was kind of frightening when she thought of her being able to sneak around the house. She hoped that she might get used to it very soon. Shrugging those ideas off, she hurried into the bathroom to shower and dress. Hopefully, she would be ready on time.

She filled the tub with warm water and bubble bath. She looked at the seashells on the wallpaper and thought of Hawaii and her honeymoon. She enjoyed the warm water and stayed a moment longer than she had planned. Hastily, she styled her hair, put on make-up and dressed in a pair of dark green slacks and a gray tee-shirt.

Outside of her room, the hall was dimly lit. She knew that she had taken longer than half an hour to get ready so she decided to hurry to the right of the stairway. A few steps down, she noticed a door open that had been locked yesterday. Adrian said it was a surprise and it was not ready to be seen until after their honeymoon. She could not resist taking a peek inside it.

The room was empty except for a number of large boxes. Printed on the cartons were the words, "Valley Furniture Rental". For a moment, she puzzled over why Adrian would be renting furniture. She dismissed the thought as not being too important or he had only used the boxes to help move his things into the house. Glancing at her watch, she saw how late it was and after closing the door, she rushed down the hall to the steps and down to the dining room.

Mrs. Simms was waiting for her when she finally entered the dining room. She was an imposing figure even standing at the other end of the long table. The tall woman looked stern dressed in a black dress with an over-sized dark blue sweater. Her face had the usual hard expression that Jessica had come to expect. Silently, she pointed to a chair at the far end of the table which had breakfast set out in front of it.

Jessica made her excuses and obediently sat down in the chair. The housekeeper removed the cover revealing a plate with buttered toast and two fried eggs. By the plate were a small glass with orange juice and a steaming cup of coffee. The older woman left the room without a word.

"Well, at least, I can eat my meal in peace. Her face is enough to curdle milk. I sure hope she gets a bit friendlier soon," she thought as she fixed her coffee and began to eat her breakfast. She wished Adrian was sharing this meal with her. Quickly, she ate and went back to her room to get dressed.

She sat down in front of the vanity and began to brush her hair, daydreaming about life after her wedding. No more helping nasty customers in the deli, no more lonely nights, no more...

A car horn startled her back to reality. "Oh, no!" She cried looking at the clock, "A half hour gone by all ready! Where's my dress, my shoes?"

She began to dash around the room, picking up shoes, clothes and tossing them on the bed. Just then, the door of her room opened and Mrs. Simms stood staring at the disarray of the room and her. The woman's face had an even more stern expression and Jessica felt a sudden fear of her, towering over as she did. Her manner made her feel that the housekeeper believed her to be an intruder in the house instead of her future mistress. Without waiting for a word, she swept into the room and began to pick clothes and brushes off the floor.

"Oh, Mrs. Simms, I'm almost ready, really I am." Jessica stammered as she bent down to pick a shoe off the floor. "It's just that I am excited about today and I was daydreaming. After all, it is my wedding day and it only happens once and..."

"Well, that may be, but if there is going to be a wedding today, I'd better help you. Not that it would be any of my concern if it was called off."

Jessica felt as if this older woman had physically slapped her. All she could say was a whispered, "I'm sorry you feel that way."

Mrs. Simms did not seem to hear as she continued picking up clothes and scolding. "You sit down there while I go and get your dress out of the closet. Please try and get your mind on getting ready and not some silly day dream. I have got to go and help Mr. Simms put your bags in the car and then I'll be back up to help you fix your hair. It needs a lot of work, I can see that. Just make sure you are dressed when I get back."

With that rebuke, she marched in triumph out of the room, slamming the door hard. Jessica was trembling as she put on her dress.

"That woman! She acts like she's the owner of the house instead of Adrian. After we're married, she'll have to be more civil to me or out she goes! If my mother were here, she wouldn't dare treat me like that. I wish she were here now."

Sighing, she put on the dress that Adrian had picked out for her to wear. She began to gaze at herself in the full length mirror and felt pleased at what she saw. The navy suit with a clean white blouse was stylish for her and her shoes were also navy with a short heel. Adrian did not think white was necessary and the suit would be more comfortable for travel than her blue dress as they were going straight to the airport after the ceremony. She had to admit that even though she was disappointed in not having a wedding gown, she did look good in the suit. The finishing touch was the gold cross that was her mother's last gift to her. It was a link to her that made Jessica feel as if her mother was somehow with her on the most important day of her life. After fixing the necklace around her neck, she sat down at the vanity and waited for the housekeeper.

All too soon, Mrs. Simms marched into the room without bothering to knock. Jessica breathed a sigh of relief, as she had been able to be dressed and seated at the vanity before her entry. With only a nod in her direction, the older woman picked up the hairbrush and began to style her hair.

Looking in the mirror at the housekeeper, Jessica asked, "Mrs. Simms, do you know much about Adrian's family? He never talks about his parents or anything."

"It's not my place to know anything about his background. All I know is that his father was a horrible man who had little time for him when he was young. Now he has no time for..." She hesitated and cleared her throat. "That is not important now. I'm not one to gossip about my employer. If he wants you to know, he'll tell you but you won't hear anything from me. It's none of my business."

Jessica noticed a nervous look on the housekeeper's face as she finished combing out her hair. She acted as she felt that she had said too much. Maybe this woman knew more about Adrian than she was willing to say.

Before Jessica could say anything else, Mr. Simms opened the door. "The car is packed! We'd better leave right now or we won't be on time. Mr. Daniels doesn't like to be kept waiting especially if it is bringing his bride-to-be to the courthouse."

"All right, William, we're ready! Hurry, Miss Jessica!"

Mrs. Simms grabbed her right arm and Mr. Simms held on to her left arm and in this manner they almost dragged her down the stairs. It seemed to Jessica that they were in an incredible hurry to see her married to Adrian even though they had only worked for him a short period of time. She was pushed into the back seat of the car and the older couple jumped into the front seat. Mr. Simms accelerated down the driveway in a flurry of pebbles and leaves. Were they on their way to a fire or a wedding? Catching her breath, she settled down into the plush seat of the car and tried not to notice just how fast he was driving.

Soon they slowed down as they drove into the downtown section of the city. As usual there were several cars parked around the courthouse and they circled the block a number of times. After the fourth circle, a car pulled out of a space in front of the steps.

As he was helping her out of the car, she suddenly thought, "Am I doing the right thing? I hardly know the man I've agreed to marry. Perhaps I should..."

She never finished that thought for as soon as she hesitated, the couple took her arms and began to maneuver her up the steps to the door of the courthouse.

"Now, Miss Jessica, you don't want to keep Mr. Daniels waiting, do you! We're right on time now."

It was if their words became a wake-up call for her. Of course she wanted to marry Adrian. They were in love and were supposed to be man and wife. Shaking off their hands, she went into the courthouse and into the office of the justice of the peace.

To her relief, Norma Jean and her husband were standing at the front of the room. The two friends greeted each other with a hug. Norma Jean whispered "You look lovely, honey. I'm praying you'll be real happy. Don't forget me, you hear. Anytime you need to talk, you can call. Here's a little gift that will bless you and your marriage."

She handed her a maroon leather bound Bible. Inside the front cover were the words, "God bless Jessica and Adrian on their Wedding Day. May this book be the center of their life together." It was signed by Norma Jean and the rest of the employees of Clyde's Deli.

"They wanted to be here but it wouldn't work out to close the deli today. Their thoughts are with both of you."

Before she could reply, Adrian came over and said, "We're ready to start now, darling. You can talk to your friends after the ceremony. The justice of the peace has a tight schedule."

Taking her arm, he led her up to the front where a elderly man in a black suit was standing. The justice of the peace motioned where everyone should stand and began the ceremony.

Jessica barely heard all the words but she did reply in all the right places. Her full attention was on the man she was marrying. He was dressed in a dark blue suit with a white shirt and a light blue tie with black stripes. She thought about how handsome he looked and just smiled. When he looked into her eyes, she saw a smile and a glimmering glimpse of his love for her. Twice during the ceremony, he glanced at her and winked.

When the justice of the peace pronounced them to be man and wife, Adrian clasped her close and gave her a passionate kiss. She felt her face begin to burn as the kiss seemed to go on for a long time. Still she was sorry when he stopped and stepped back. He smiled and turned away to shake the hand of the justice. "Thank you, sir. It was a good service."

"Of course, Mr. Daniels, and may I be the first to congratulate you and your new bride. I hope you will be very happy together."

"Yes, you have been very kind," she said as she shook the justice's hand and accepted his words of congratulation. Next she turned and received hugs from her friend and her husband.

Norma Jean had tears in her eyes as she said, "Be happy now, honey. It'll all work out. I'm so happy for you."

"We better go now, Jessica. We have a plane to catch." Adrian was behind her and holding on the her elbow. He reached over to shake the hands of the two people and thanked them for coming. "We do have so little time before our flight leaves. You understand. We'll be in touch as soon as we get back from our honeymoon. Good-bye"

He pulled her toward the door and she only had time to say a quick good-bye and wave to her friends. Soon they were outside and running down the steps to the car. Mrs. Simms was in the front seat and Mr. Simms was holding the door open for them. In only a moment, they were inside and driving away to the airport.

As they were leaving, Jessica saw Norma Jean and Sam waving to them. She waved to them before she turned to look at her husband. "Well, now, how does it feel to be Mrs. Daniels?"

"Mrs. Daniels! Oh, Adrian, I'm so happy to have that as my name. You have no idea how happy I am now."

CHAPTER 9

It was a bright, warm July day as the light poured through her bedroom window and woke Jessica. She turned to see if Adrian was awake, but his side of the bed was empty. Hearing the shower, she decided she would lie in bed for a while longer and wait for him to come out. Perhaps he would have few plans, and they could be together all day.

She smiled as she thought of the two weeks since her wedding. She still could not believe all of this was happening to her. Hawaii had been a dream come true and they were so happy just being together there. She had wished that somehow time would go on forever, but at least she would always treasure her memories.

Days were spent on the beach and sometimes on a sightseeing tour. Her favorite spot were the volcanoes, so full of fire and light. All their time was spent together except for one day when Adrian went deep-sea fishing. He had tried to persuade her to come with him, but she refused for she knew she would get sea sick. She did not try to keep him from going, even though she wanted to do just that. She felt that he should have some fun.

The nights were even more beautiful, for they were such romantic times with candlelight dinners on the terrace of their room or strolls along a moonlit beach. While they were alone, he gave all of his attention to her and thrilled her with his love. In their room at night, he was the ever passionate lover, and she felt that no two people could be more in love than they. His words spoke of his love her and many promises were made as they lay together every night.

In the morning, she took out the Bible that Norma Jean gave her and she felt like she had found an old friend. The day that Adrian was on the fishing boat, she sat down under an umbrella on the beach and read through the Gospel of John, which had been her mother's favorite. The more she read, the more she was convicted by the words that her life was not what it should be. She read, "For God so loved the world, that He gave His only begotten Son, that whosoever believeth in Him should not perish but have everlasting life." She remembered that it was the verse that brought her to accepting Jesus at a revival meeting so long ago. The rest of the book spoke so much of God's love that she vowed to try to read the Bible more and return to church. Perhaps she could persuade Adrian to accompany her. That night, she tried sharing what she had discovered with him, but he was too tired to talk.

Her memories were interrupted by his reappearance from the bathroom dressed in a gray suit. "Oh, you're awake, Darling. I tried not to wake you so that you could get some more rest after that late flight last night." He spoke very casually as he straightened his tie in the mirror.

"I'm fine, love. I do believe I got enough rest. Are you going out? I thought we could spend some time together. We need to look over the house and make decisions about redecorating as you promised I could do. Couldn't we do it today?"

"Hey now, Mrs. Daniels, we just spent two whole weeks together. Remember? I have a business to run and there's no telling what has been happening to my company since

I've been gone. My assistant is a good man but..." His voice trailed off as he went back into the bathroom so she was not able to hear the rest of what he had said.

At first she felt let down over his going back to work, but she realized that he was right. "Adrian, maybe I could stop by your office and go with you to lunch. I've never been there and I'd like to see just where you spend your time away from me. What do you say?"

Adrian rushed out of the bathroom with such an alarmed look on his face that she was startled for a moment. "No, no, you can't do that!" he stammered, but then seemed to regain his composure. "No, that's not necessary, my dear. I already have an engagement for lunch, strictly business, you know."

"Well, can I come down another time? I really do want to be involved in all of your life, even business."

"To be quite frank with you, Jessica, I do not want you coming down to my office at any time. My wife need not to concern herself with my company or investments. You'll have plenty to keep you occupied running this household and entertaining my guests and business associates. Do you understand?" As he spoke, his voice grew so cold and sharp that Jessica shivered and pulled the covers up to her chin.

In a very meek voice, she replied, "All right, darling. If that's what you want, but I just don't see..."

"Promise me that you'll forget about coming to the office!" His gaze had not lost all of it's frosty nature as he looked directly into her eyes.

"Yes, yes, I promise. I won't ever mention it again," she mumbled sheepishly and looked away from his eyes. "Will you be eating breakfast here with me?"

"No, I'll get something downtown later. I'll be home this evening. Goodbye," As he said this, he bent down and lightly kissed her cheek, not at all the passionate kiss that she had hoped to receive. He seemed different to her, just like the man she knew before Hawaii.

"Wasn't that odd," she said aloud as she got out of bed and looked out the window. Raising the window, she wanted to clear her head with some fresh air for the old feeling of uneasiness came flooding back into her mind. "He was really frightened for a moment that I would come to his office. Could he be hiding something from me?"

Just then, the front door opened and Adrian came out, followed by Mrs. Simms. From her vantage point, she could see and hear them quite clearly. She started to back away from the window until she heard her husband say in a rather impatient voice, "I don't know why you are so upset. Remember, we decided on this months ago."

"All right, I know what I said I would do, but I don't have to like it. Do I?"

"No, you don't, but just remember the benefits." He spoke in a very soothing and loving manner and even put his arm's around the housekeeper's shoulders. "It shouldn't be too much longer. I've got to go now or I'll be late for my appointment. Don't worry." She was shocked to see him kiss her on the cheek before he got into his car and left.

Leaving the window, Jessica had to sit down on the bed, for her knees felt suddenly weak. Just what was that all about? People did not normally kiss their housekeepers before going to work, did they? She did not know what to do, but perhaps she should try to find out one way or another.

As she sat back on the bed pondering these questions, she did not hear the light knocking on the door, and when she did look up, Mrs. Simms was standing in front of her staring at the open window. "I'm sorry for barging in like I did, Ma'am, but I did knock. Here, let me shut the window for you. Breakfast will be ready in twenty minutes. Call if you need me for something." Quickly, she closed the window and left the room.

Jessica shrugged her shoulders, and thought "She seemed a little nervous about the open window and she was more polite than she has been before now. I wonder what caused that? Probably nothing, but I better keep my eyes and ears open from now on." After getting dressed, she went down to breakfast, but with many questions hanging in her mind.

At breakfast, Mrs. Simms was unusually polite again, and even sat down with her for a moment as she finished her coffee. "What would you care to do today? If you wish, we could plan the meals for the week. Mr. Simms is planning to go to the grocery store this afternoon."

"Yes, that would be fine after I finish my coffee."

"Very good, Ma'am. I'll go and make up your room while you do that. While I'm there, I'll see that your luggage is unpacked and everything is put in its proper place."

Mrs. Simms left the room, and Jessica felt more comfortable with her gone. While sipping her coffee, she wondered just how she could get her questions answered and put the doubts about her husband to rest once and for all. "I know just what to do," she said aloud, "I could go visit my friends at the deli. It will be good to see them again, especially Norma Jean. Maybe she can help. Besides, I need to tell someone about Hawaii. Won't they be jealous."

As she left the dining room, she noticed Mrs. Simms putting the receiver back down on the hall telephone and going up the stairs. Who was she calling? She could not remember hearing the phone ring.

Just then, the telephone did ring and Jessica decided to answer it. The voice was Adrian's and he said, "Jessica? Why didn't Mrs. Simms answer the phone?"

"She's busy. Did you want to speak to her or me?"

"Well, Darling, I wanted to speak to you and apologize for my behavior this morning. Also, my luncheon date was cancelled, and I thought we could go to lunch together. What do you say to that?"

"That sounds wonderful, sweetheart. I had wanted to go and see my old friends at the deli and visit for a while."

"Good. Tell Mr. Simms to bring you into town around noon and we can meet at the deli and have our lunch there. But I would like you to give a message to Mrs. Simms for me."

"Oh, all right. Go ahead."

"Tell Mrs. Simms that the stocks we discussed this morning have begun to go up just like I said they would. So she need not worry about them anymore, and her savings should double in the next year. Can you remember all that? The only reason that I want you to tell her right away is she was so distraught about it this morning. I guess she was afraid of losing her savings."

"I'll be sure to tell her. Is that all?"

"Yes, darling. You should have seen just how worried and scared she was when I was leaving for the office. I had given her the tip a few months ago and we had both invested a lot of money in the stock. Then when the stock fell yesterday, she was frantic. I had to comfort her to get her to calm down and stop worrying before she would let me leave for the office. Now it looks like we did the right thing. Anyhow I have to go, so I'll see you at noon. Make sure that you tell Mrs. Simms right away."

"Of course. Goodbye, Adrian," Jessica hung up the telephone and stood in the hallway for a few minutes. "So he was comforting her over the fear of losing her life's savings", she thought, "I can see why he was so nice to her. What else could it be? But I wonder..."

Going up the stairs, she called to Mrs. Simms to let her know what Adrian had said and that she would be going into town after all. She decided to put the morning's events out of her mind. She was probably putting too much importance into it.

Chapter 10

The sun was shining brightly through the window of his car as Jonathan Miner drove down Interstate 40. Earlier that day as he was getting dressed, he had taken a long look at himself in the mirror. His light brown hair seemed to be getting a little thinner and he realized there was little he could do about that. However, his six foot, two frame seemed to be heavier than he remembered. "Hmm, looks like I could use some exercise - maybe some time off." He murmured as he finished dressing in a gray pin-striped suit. "Not too bad, but these pants seem a little tight."

As he was leaving his apartment, the day was so lovely and warm, he toyed with the idea of taking the day off. Maybe he could call the office and tell them he was sick. Then he could play some golf or go fishing at a stream in the mountains that was just full of trout. However, the more he thought of ways to get the day off, he realized all of them would be deceitful and being a Christian, he knew it was wrong.

So he got in his car and headed towards the office. As he was driving, he felt bad about what he had almost done and he prayed, "Dear Lord, I'm sorry that I almost lied. Please forgive me. Thank you for this beautiful day. Be with me at work and help me to serve you today." He felt better and even had a feeling that something special would happen to him at work that day.

Upon arriving at the office in downtown Winston-Salem, Jonathan found a note waiting for him at the reception desk. It was from his boss, Mr. Cranston and said-"Come to my office immediately." He had been working for the law firm of Garland, Emery and Mason for two years since graduating from law school. This was the first time he had been summoned to the boss's office. As he knocked on the door, he felt a knot tie up in his stomach, and he silently asked the Lord to help him.

Mr. Cranston, the office manager, rose from his chair and motioned for Jonathan to sit down by his desk. Also sitting in the office were the two active partners in the firm, Phillip Emery and Samuel Mason. All three men were in their late fifties, and except for Mr. Mason, were tall and muscular like retired athletes. Mr. Mason was just the opposite as he was short and thin. Jonathan had never seen all three of the men together and had only spoken briefly to the two partners. It made him feel even more nervous as he sat down.

"Well I'm sure you're wondering why you're here, Jonathan. Please be at ease, we have an assignment for you. Mr. Emery will explain." Mr. Cranston spoke with a smile which put Jonathan somewhat at ease, and then sat down.

Mr. Emery stood and sat on the edge of the desk in front of Jonathan. "Mr. Garland, our retired partner, called us yesterday. It seems he needs one of our young associates to drive down to his house in Hickory and help him on a case. Right now, most of our other associates are busy on cases except for you, Mr. Miner. We're not really sure what the assignment will be, but it must be important. Would you be interested?"

"Well-er-of course, I would. Just tell me what I need to do," Jonathan said. None of the newer associates had ever met the "old man" as everyone called Mr. Garland. He did have a reputation among the older staff as being hard in business. Anyhow, this did seem like a big break for him.

"Good, Mr. Miner," Mr. Emery continued, "We were sure that you were the one for this job for Mr. Cranston recommended you to us. The first thing you need to do is go home and pack a bag, for you will be out of town for at least a couple of weeks, maybe longer. Then you will drive down to Hickory to Mr. Garland's and he will explain the rest to you. Do you have any questions?"

"Yes, I do. Do you have any idea what Mr. Garland wants?"

"No, I'm afraid we do not." Mr. Mason spoke from the other side of the room where he was looking out the window. "He just asked if we could spare one of our associates for a few weeks. He's always been rather mysterious about his business."

"Now, Sam, we don't need to bring that up," Mr. Emery said as he sat down next to Jonathan. "If you don't have any other questions, you can be on your way, Mr. Miner. Just be sure to stop by the reception desk and pick up directions and an expense check. All your expenses will be paid either by the firm or Mr. Garland himself. Anyhow, good luck to you!" As he finished speaking, he rose and shook Jonathan's hand as he ushered him to the door.

At home, Jonathan threw some things in a suitcase and in an hour, was on his way to Hickory. Some questions did bother him. What did Mr. Mason mean by mysterious and did he really seem upset at the mention of Mr. Garland? Why did they all wish him good luck? Would he really need it?

The day was so pleasant that he put those doubts out of his mind. With the radio playing, the trip seemed short and soon he was pulling off at the exit to Hickory. The directions he had were detailed and easy to follow. In only a few short minutes, he stopped in front of a large colonial style house on a quiet street. As he was ringing the doorbell, he could feel the sweat rolling down the back of his neck. "I hope the 'old man' doesn't see how nervous I am."

Presently, the door was opened by an elderly man, around five foot six or so with gray hair and dark blue eyes. he definitely looked the part of a butler in a black suit. "Are you Mr.Miner? We have been expecting you. Please come in." He spoke in a heavy British accent but no smile showed on his worn face. "Mr. Garland will see you in a few moments. Please be seated in the parlor. I will announce your arrival." He pointed to a room off to the right of the entrance hall. Then he slowly mounted the steep steps and was gone.

Jonathan entered the parlor expecting to see antique furniture but he was surprised to see it was decorated like a hunting cabin with pine furniture. On the walls were game trophies, deer and fish with many pictures of various game and hunting dogs. One picture that caught his eye was of a young man in hunting gear surrounded by a pack of beagles. The man was of medium built with light colored hair and a large mustache. The caption read, "Mr. Thomas Garland and his beagles" and it was dated October 19, 1926. Before he could look closely at any more pictures, the butler told him that Mr. Garland would see him now in his bedroom upstairs.

Entering the bedroom, he noticed the room was decorated in the same manner as the parlor downstairs with rustic furniture and game trophies on the wall. These trophies, he noticed were exotic ones that a person might bag in Africa or Asia. He almost expected to see the man in the picture standing there. However, in the dim light, he saw sitting up in the bed an old man who looked ill and tired. His face was puffy and a white scruff of a beard was evident as he had not shaved for a couple of days. A few white hairs still lingered around the ears, but the top was shiny and bald. Could this be the same man in the picture? Of course, he realized that picture was taken long ago, and this man had aged as all men must.

A young man in a sport shirt and khakis stood up as Jonathan entered the room. He was tall, about six feet, with brown curly hair and darkly tanned skin. Before the young man could speak, the old man in the bed said, "Oh, here you are, Mr. Miner. Please, both of you sit yourselves down. This fellow here is Jack Sampson and you're Jonathan Miner." Jonathan shook his hand and they both sat down.

"I saw you admiring my trophies. Are you a hunter, too, boy?"

Jonathan felt more at ease with this man for he seemed more like a country farmer than a retired lawyer. "Well, yes, Mr. Garland. I've done a little hunting and fishing when I can get the chance, but not as successfully as you." The three of them talked of hunting, fishing, and hunting dogs for quite a while.

Soon, the "old man" cut off the talk of the outdoors with, "Well, son, I didn't bring you two fellows here to swap stories. I got a very important job for you two.

"Years ago, I was very sick. My doctors thought I was fixing to die. What do they know? Ha, ha! I sure showed them up, 'cause I'm still here and some of them aren't. Anyhow, my niece, who is a nurse, came to my house and took real good care of me. Her name's Olivia. When I was better, she left, and moved up north to Virginia somewhere. I want you two boys to find her for me. Are you game to try? I'll pay you a good sum and all expenses. What do you say?"

"Well, sure, Mr. Garland! But we'll need more details than that," Jack spoke up quickly before Jonathan could say a word. "How about you?" he turned to Jonathan with a questioning look.

"I suppose so, Mr. Garland, but I'd need to know more also." Jonathan managed to say. He was beginning to get a little curious about the whole setup.

Mr. Garland's face brightened up and he said, "That's fine. I just knew you'd do it. First off, Jonathan, Jack here is one of the best new private investigators in Hickory. He's helped me on quite a few cases recently." At these words, Jack stood up and bowed with a grand flourish.

"Oh, sit down, Jack! Anyhow, Jonathan is a new associate with my old firm in Winston-Salem. I'm glad they sent you. Didn't seem like they wanted to do it since I've not talked to them much lately, especially that old "kill- joy" Mason. Never did get along with him. That's why I didn't tell them too much - none of their business if you ask me. Well, enough of that - the introductions been done, now we can get down to business."

For the next hour, Mr. Garland told them all that he knew about the nurse he wanted them to find. Most of his recollections were patchy but some he seemed to remember as if they had only happened yesterday. Jonathan did his best to take careful notes, but at times Mr. Garland's mind would wander to other subjects. When this happened, Jack was always able to steer him back to the subject. In fact, their relationship seemed to be more like a father to son than a lawyer to a hired private investigator. Every so often, he was forced to stop for a coughing spell, but when he had some water and rested for a moment, he continued.

"Well, boys, that's about all I can tell you. You might ask William some questions. He was working for me when my niece lived here, so he might know something. He got on really well with the little girl. Did I mention her? Such a lovely and friendly girl, just like her mother. She and I had such wonderful talks and I'm sure she helped me get well almost as much as her mother. Now, what was her name? Was it Jenny? No - no, that's not it!" There was a pause as the old man tried to recall the name. Suddenly, he said, "Oh yes, now I remember, it was Jessica! I sure would like to see her again but..."

He never finished for William came into the room with Mr. Garland's medicine and announced that they would have to leave because he needed to rest. "You boys find them for me, Olivia and Jessica. Report back to me often, you hear."

These last words seemed to tire him out and he sank back down on the bed. The two men quietly left and went down to the parlor to talk.

"My, but the `old man' seems to be in bad health," Jonathan said as they sat down.

"He's dying, poor old fellow - only a few months left to live. I'll sure miss him," Jack murmured as he stifled back a slight choke in his voice, "The doctors say that the cancer has spread too far to operate."

"It seems like you and him are really close. Have you known him long?"

"Mr. Garland is like a father to me. Ever since I came here to Hickory three years ago, he's helped me out. I don't know how long the firm would have kept me except for Mr. Garland insisting on me to help his cases, as few as they were. I'd do anything for him."

"Do you know if he has any other family?"

"I've never met them, but he has a wife and son. They've been divorced for quite a few years, and they never come around here. Mr. Garland hardly ever mentions them and I know very little about either of them. But that's not important, is it?"

Before Jonathan could answer, the butler came into the room with a tray of sandwiches and soft drinks. "Mr. Garland insisted that you chaps have some refreshment. Please help yourself. Also, I have prepared a room for you, Mr. Miner, and I have taken the liberty of taking your things up there. Dinner is at eight."

As William turned to leave the room, Jack jumped up and said, "Do sit down, old boy, we have a few questions for you." The butler reluctantly sat down across form the two men. He was able to tell them some more facts that Mr. Garland had not mentioned. The most important thing being the name of the nursing agency that sent Mr. Garland's niece there. Excusing himself, the butler left the two men alone to eat and talk.

While they ate, the discussed what they had learned and planned their next move. After a half hour, Jack said, "It's too late in the day to get started. I had better run along, pack a suitcase and get a good night's rest. Our first stop tomorrow will be the nursing agency, and it's a long drive to Raleigh. I'll pick you up around five thirty tomorrow morning. Perhaps they'll have a forwarding address for her. Anyhow, one way or another, we've got to find Olivia Weston and her daughter, Jessica!"

CHAPTER 11

Jonathan was sitting on the couch in the parlor talking to a young and most attractive woman. Glancing over to the other side of the room, her mother in a nurse's uniform was reading a health magazine. Smiling, the young woman whispered, "Where have you been all my life?"

Before he could answer, someone was knocking loudly on a door. "Mr. Miner, it's five o'clock. Time to get up!"

Opening his eyes, he was not sure of his surroundings in the dim light. As he rubbed the sleep from his eyes, he remembered that he was at Mr. Garland's house. He was somewhat disappointed to realize he had only been dreaming about the woman and her mother.

"All right, William, I'm awake. Thank you." He called out to the butler as he sat up in bed.

"Very good, sir. Breakfast will be ready in half an hour when Mr. Sampson arrives." So saying, he walked softly away from the door.

The memory of the dream still bothered him as he stretched and got out of bed. Was it Jessica and her mother Olivia that he saw in his mind or was it just wishful thinking on his part? After all, he was not getting any younger at the age of thirty two. Perhaps the thought of finding a missing loved one had given him romantic visions of also finding someone for himself. She would be in her late twenties now if the dates he had been given were correct. While he dressed, he wondered what these two women were like and if they would like him. Many questions were in his mind as he sat down to breakfast, that he was really eager to get started even at this early hour.

As he was beginning to eat his grapefruit, Jack Sampson breezed into the room. "Hello, Jonathan. Did you sleep well? I'm really hungry." Taking a seat next to Jonathan, he literally dove into his grapefruit.

Jonathan noticed that Jack still did not seem appropriately dressed in any kind of professional manner. The jeans and striped sports shirt that he was wearing clashed with Jonathan's light blue suit. In his mind, he wondered how this partnership could possibly work.

Jack did not seem to notice Jonathan's silence but continued talking, "Yes sir, we have a long drive to get to Raleigh today. I figured we would go in my car, if you don't mind. When we get to Raleigh, we can find a room and I'll change into a more business like person. How's that sound to you?"

"Sounds fine to me." Jonathan said with some relief. He felt as if Jack had somehow known what he was thinking and a little guilty for jumping to conclusions about his partner too soon.

Just at that point, William returned with a tray of scrambled eggs, bacon and muffins with two cups of coffee. As he laid the food on the table, he said, "Mr. Garland had wanted to join you this morning, but he did not sleep well last night. I convinced him to take his nourishment in his room later this morning. He did instruct me to give you this." Picking up a large envelope from the side board, he handed it to Jonathan and left the room.

In the envelope was a picture of a woman in a nurse's uniform, young girl, and a younger Mr. Garland, plus a smaller envelope. On the envelope was a note written in a scrawled manner which he read aloud, "Here is the only picture I have of Olivia and Jessica. Please take special care of it. Inside you will find some cash to get you started. Good luck." It was signed, Thomas S. Garland. Opening the smaller envelope, he was startled to find five hundred dollars in twenties and fifties.

"Well, at least we have some spending money." Jack said in between bites of food. Both of them studied the picture, but after a few minutes Jack concentrated only on his breakfast while Jonathan continued to stare at the picture. To him, the mother was a very attractive woman with a worn face, even though she was smiling. The little girl was pretty with a bright face of childhood that made her seem so sweet and innocent. He wondered if she looked anything like her mother now, because she would be a very attractive woman. In his heart, he hoped that she did.

Finishing their breakfast, the two rose to leave. William was waiting for them at the door. He had already placed Jonathan's luggage by the door. "Remember sirs, Mr. Garland is extremely anxious to find these two women. He realizes he only has a short period of time to live now and it would do him good to see Olivia and Jessica again. It is almost as if he believes they can make him well once more. Anyhow, he wants you to call him collect every night to report your findings. Goodbye, gentlemen and God speed."

"Thanks," Jack said, patting him on the back. "We'll find them as fast as we can. Tell him not to worry."

Going out the door, Jonathan was not surprised at seeing Jack's car. It was a late model sports sedan in a bright orange. As he helped with the suitcases, he hoped that Jack was a safe driver. However as they drove out of town, he realized he had little to fear on that account.

The drive to Raleigh was a long one, but quite pleasant as the day was warm and sunny. They talked of hunting and other sports for the first part of the trip. Later in the day, their conversation centered only on the case and the questions they hoped would be answered at the agency. After checking into a motel, they got directions from the desk clerk and headed for the nursing agency.

Behind the desk at the nursing agency was an attractive woman wearing large eyeglasses. Smiling, she asked if she could be of service to them. "Well, yes. My name is Jack Sampson and this is Jonathan Miner. We are trying to locate a nurse who worked for you a few years ago. Our client was one of her patients as well as her uncle and he is anxious to find her before he dies. Can you be of help to us?"

"I'm sure we can, but you'll have to tell me the name and how long ago she was employed by us."

"Her name is Olivia Weston and it was around twenty years ago. Do you still have those records?"

"Twenty years? I'll have to go back and look in our outdated files. It should only take a few minutes."

The two men found seats in the waiting room. All the magazines were months old and of little interest to them. The few minutes began to stretch into many minutes and they wondered if she would even find the information. Finally, she reappeared with an older woman whom they assumed was her supervisor.

The older woman spoke first, "I'm Mrs. Rider, Miss Clark's supervisor. She says you are looking for an Olivia Weston. Why do you wish to find her?"

"Our client, Mr. Thomas Garland of Hickory, who was her patient twenty years ago and her uncle wishes to see her again before he dies. I'm sad to say that he is in failing health right now. Is there some problem?"

"Oh, no! It is just unusual to have two inquiries about the same person in so short a time. A man was here about nine months ago looking for Mrs. Weston who also said he was representing a relative. I recall him so well because he was in such a hurry and was so nasty to the clerk, so I ended up giving him the information. I was just curious, that's all. I'm sorry if I delayed you." Turning to Miss Clark, she added, "Give them whatever facts they need."

"The last address we have on Olivia Weston is this one in Richmond, Virginia. Also, here is the name of the hospital where she was working when she left here. Of course, all of this is twenty years old, so I can't guarantee that she'll still be there."

Jonathan carefully copied down the address and hospital and said, "Thank you. This will help."

Once they were outside and in his car, Jack commented, "It's not much, but it's a start. Tomorrow we'll have to catch a plane to Richmond. Then we'll see."

"What do you think of the other inquiry of her whereabouts? It sounds a little suspicious to me."

"Probably just a coincidence, that's all. She was a good nurse and others were grateful. What else could it be? Besides, it has nothing to do with us."

"Yeah, I guess you're right." Jonathan replied. He hoped that Jack was right, but something told him that this could be trouble for them later.

Chapter 12

Walking through the corridors of the hospital, the two men looked for the personnel office. After getting directions from a fourth person, they were sure they could find it. "Hospitals have a way of getting a person lost." Jack commented as they made yet another turn.

"Right," was Jonathan's only reply for he was thinking about his conversation last night with William. He had wanted to speak to Mr. Garland directly but was informed that he was resting. William did tell him that he had become weaker during the day. Both men were worried after he hung up that Mr. Garland would die before they could even find the Westons.

"Hey, here it is - we found it," Jack interrupted Jonathan's thoughts as they finally stood in front of the door marked, Personnel Office. "Let's hope they can help us. Just let me do all the talking. Usually these people tend to be closed-mouthed about information, but I know how to handle it."

The man behind the first desk glanced up as they walked into the office. With a look of annoyance, he asked in a rather cold voice, "May I help you in some way?"

Jack stepped forward and replied in a stern and authoritative manner, "Yes, you may, my good man. We need some information on one of your nurses and we're in quite a hurry so please don't keep us waiting. Here's the name of the woman we need to locate." He handed the clerk a slip of paper while keeping a firm and steady gaze on him.

Looking somewhat confused, the clerk took the paper and left the room. Jack chuckled and sat down by the desk. "That should get us some results right quick. All these clerks understand is someone giving orders. Did you see his expression change? Do sit down, Jonathan, and stop looking so gloomy. It might take a while."

"I just hope you know what you're doing. You were a little hard on that fellow. Don't you think?"

"To get these people to do anything, you have to be firm. Let them know that they have to help you and they fall all over themselves doing it. Just wait - you'll see."

Jonathan nodded and glanced around the outer office. Behind a counter on the far side of the room, he noticed a young woman watching them. She was a small woman with a rather plain face who blushed and looked away. It had seemed she was very interested in what they had been saying to the clerk.

Just then, the clerk reappeared, followed by another man. Both of them approached with solemn faces, but were not carrying any folders. The other man spoke first, "Excuse me, but my clerk says you want information from our files. Do you have any authorization to see these records?"

Jack was startled for a moment, but soon regained his own air of authority. "We are working for a client in North Carolina who wishes to contact this particular nurse. He is one of her only living relatives and is now dying. He wishes to see her again. Is there some problem?"

"As a matter of fact there is a problem. You cannot come into this office and demand confidential information just like that. I will have to see some authorization before I release any files for anybody. Is that clear?" Not giving them any chance to reply, he handed Jack the paper and marched back into his office.

The clerk moved to the door and stood nervously holding it open for them to leave. Jonathan could see that Jack was speechless for once, so he said, "Look, we're sorry if we were rude and bossy, but we must contact this nurse. Our client is an old man who only wishes to see his niece again before he dies. Isn't there some way you could help us? It would mean a lot to make a dying man's last days a little happier."

"There is no way I can be of any help to you. Please leave or I'll be forced to call security and have you escorted off the premises," was the curt reply of the clerk. The two men only shrugged their shoulders and left. As they were leaving, Jonathan noticed the shy young woman had also left the room.

"It seems like your way didn't help at all. Now we have to try something else." Jonathan admonished him as they stood outside the office. "Perhaps I could find a lawyer here in town to..."

His words were interrupted by the young woman from the personnel office beckoning from the hall. Curiously, they followed her around the corner to another hallway. She motioned them to keep quiet and sit down with her on a bench in the hall. She seemed nervous and kept looking around to see if anyone was watching.

With her voice in a low, uneasy whisper, she said, "I couldn't help overhearing your conversation with my supervisor and I thought maybe I could help you. Were you telling the truth about the man dying and all?"

Jonathan smiled for the young woman looked very frightened and tense, and he wanted her to feel more at ease. He said, "Of course we told the truth. All my partner and I want to do is find one nurse and make our client happy. But how can you help us?"

"The other man could have helped, but he has already been in trouble for giving out information. I also have access to all the files and I could get it for you."

At this suggestion, Jack became more alert and commented, "Could you really? That would be just great. How soon would you be able to get the file?"

Before she could answer, Jonathan interrupted with, "But couldn't you get in trouble for this? We want the information badly, but not if it costs you. It's not worth that. We could probably get some kind of court order in a few days or so."

"Well, yes, I could lose my job if I was caught. But I was hoping you would be willing to pay me something for it. Like - well - er - maybe a hundred dollars." While she was speaking, she looked away from them towards the end of the corridor.

"Now, wait a minute," Jonathan declared, "We can't pay you to take those files. That's not honest and we..."

Jack gave him a shove that almost knocked him off the bench as he interrupted. "Don't mind him, Miss, we couldn't give you that much, but how about fifty? Here's the name of the nurse we wish to contact. How soon can we meet?" With that he gave Jonathan a look that told him not to say anything else.

Rising, the young woman whispered, "I have to get back before they notice I'm gone. My lunch break is in thirty minutes, so I'll meet you in the cafeteria. I've really got to go." Before they could speak, she moved with cat like quickness down the hall and vanished through another door.

Immediately Jack turned to his companion, "Hey, I know I blew it in the office with that mousy little clerk, but we can't turn down an offer like that. Do I have to remind you of the little time we have left?"

"No, you don't. I'm quite aware of Mr. Garland's failing condition. It's just that it seems so dishonest to bribe someone for information."

"Look, I don't care. All I want to do is the job we started, no matter what it takes or costs. If you're still with me, let's go find the cafeteria."

Jonathan started to protest but his partner had already gone around the corner. Feeling that he better stick with him so as to keep him out of any more trouble, he ran down the hall in order to catch up.

The cafeteria was large and fortunately not crowded when they entered. Going through the line, they ordered sandwiches and soft drinks. Then they found an isolated table in a far corner and waited for their informant to show up.

They did not have to wait a long time, for soon she came into the cafeteria carrying a brown paper bag. Glancing nervously around the room, she presently made her way over to their table and sat down. "Here is the file on Olivia Weston as you wanted. Do you have the money?" Opening her purse, she handed a manila folder to Jack.

"Yeah, we do have it. Just let me copy what we need. Is there a copying machine around here?"

"There's one in the lobby, down the hall and to the left. You can't miss it."

Leaving the table, Jack took the file out of the cafeteria. Jonathan took the opportunity to speak to the young woman sitting next to him. "I am not sure what we are doing is right. However, my partner is in a hurry and will not listen to me. Don't you feel a little bit guilty? You sure don't look like a dishonest person."

Looking down at the floor, she stammered, "Ordinarily I wouldn't do such a thing, but my bills have been piling up and my salary is so small. I just had to do it. Don't you see? I had to do it."

"I don't suppose it will mean anything to you, but I hope you won't do this again. The reason I was against paying you the money is because I am a Christian and it goes against all I've been taught from the Bible. Do you understand?"

She only nodded her head silently and looked away. Seeing Jack had come back into the room, he quickly handed her a small tract. "Here, we don't have time to talk about it now, but maybe this will help you understand what being a Christian is. I'll be praying for you. Please take it and read it. I assure you it will change your life."

She took the tract, gave it a momentary glance and put it in her pocket. "I'll read it and think about what you said. Please don't judge me too harshly. I didn't know what else to do."

Jack gave her the folder and she quickly put it back in her large purse. He handed her a small envelope and said, "Here's the money. You can count it if you like. And thank you - you've really helped us."

Silently, she gathered up her things and moved to a table across the room as if she was trying to put distance between herself and what she had just done. Jack did not seem to notice for he was busy reading the copies he had made. Jonathan watched her with some sorrow, for he felt guilty about being a party to her dishonesty.

Unaware of Jonathan's feelings, Jack let out a low whistle. "Well, old boy, this record does confirm the address we were given in Raleigh. However, I see two other facts that are most interesting. One is that someone else got a court order to see this file about six months ago. But I don't believe we'll find Olivia Weston now."

"Why is that?" Jonathan was keenly interested now. "Doesn't she work here at the hospital?"

"No, I'm afraid not. You see, Olivia Weston died about two years ago."

Chapter 13

Calling Mr. Garland's house that night to report their findings of the day was the hardest thing Jonathan had yet to do. William again told him that Mr. Garland was too ill to come to the telephone. Jonathan was relieved no to be the bearer of the bad news.

"What's that you say, Mr. Miner? Olivia Weston is dead? Oh dear! What a shame. How can I tell Mr. Garland?"

"I'm not sure that you should. Perhaps you should wait till we get news on the location of her daughter which might soften the initial blow. Tomorrow we're going to their last home address."

"Very good, sir. I will tell Mr. Garland that you have not found either one as yet. There is one thing I should tell you."

"What's that William?"

"Mr. Garland is so weak now. The doctor just left a few moments ago. He does not believe he will last another week or so. I am supposed to call your law firm about the will tomorrow."

"That doesn't sound good to me. We'll call you again tomorrow night. Hopefully we will have better news about finding Jessica. Don't worry. We'll do our best to find her soon."

Early the next day, the two men went to the address from the hospital's records. The location was in an older section of the city not far from the hospital. Lining each street were townhouses of brick with small fenced yards in front of each. It was a well established and settled neighborhood with old and young people mingling on the sidewalk.

Jonathan felt that this was the kind of home he believed they would find the two women. To him, the community was a happy and generous place in which to grow. A place to grow closer to others and even closer to God was what he saw.

As he was driving, Jack was too busy looking at the street numbers to notice the houses. "Hey, there it is - number 29. This must be the place."

He parked the car in front of a townhouse with a wire fence in need of some repair and a small garden of flowers. In the front window was a sign that read, "ROOM FOR RENT". Sitting in a rocking chair was an old woman who looked like she was in her seventies. She was a plump woman wearing a faded cotton dress with an apron. Her gray hair was pulled back in a bun on top of her head and she looked like she could be anybody's ideal grandmother.

Noticing the two men by the gate staring at the house, she put her fan down and rose to her feet. Smiling, she said in a pleasant Southern drawl, "Ya'll looking for a room to rent? Got one that's real cheap."

"No, Ma'am. We're looking for someone and this is the address we were given. May we come in and talk to you?" Jack asked.

"Why, sure, come on up and sit a spell. It's always a pleasure to chat, isn't it? I'll help you if I can."

When they were all seated on the porch, the old woman spoke first. "Name's Sally Watkins. Been living here now some thirty five years so I reckon I know most people living around here. Who ya'll looking for?"

"Well, Mrs. Watkins, my name is Jonathan Miner and this is Jack Sampson. We have been hired by a man in North Carolina to locate Olivia and Jessica Weston. We were told they lived here."

"Yes - they sure did live here a couple years back. Why are you looking for them?"

"Our client, Mr. Thomas Garland, was a patient of Olivia's about twenty years ago. He is also her uncle. Now he's dying and wants to see Olivia and Jessica again. Can you help us?"

"That is such a shame, but Olivia's been dead for almost two years. Now that you mention it, she told me once - she had an uncle or some relative down in North Carolina."

She paused as if she was remembering something sad. After clearing her throat, she continued, "They were so happy living here. Then Olivia got killed in that terrible car accident. That really broke up Jessica - seemed like she was just lost without her mama. They were so close."

"What happened then, Mrs. Watkins?"

"Let's see. Jessica stayed here about a month after the funeral. I told her she could live here as long as she wanted and I'd charge a little less rent, but she got so down in spirit. She didn't know what to do. One day she just quit her job and moved out."

"Do you know where she went by any chance?"

"Don't rightly know. I reckon she just wanted to get away - get out on her own. She did leave me a month's rent, though."

Both men felt disappointed at this last bit of news for this lead seemed to be a dead end. Mrs. Watkins could see their disappointment and said, "Looks like you fellows came a long way for nothing. Don't it? Maybe I can still help you. Why don't you two come inside and let me fix you a cup of coffee. I'll try to remember something, unless you got somewhere else to go."

At the moment, neither of them could think of anywhere else to go, so they followed her through the front door and down a narrow hall. Off to the right was a small parlor, decorated in a simple style. At the left was a stairway that went straight up to a door on the second floor. At the end of the hall was a large kitchen with a long table in the middle of the room. She motioned for them to sit down at the table while she put a pot of water on the stove to boil and she sat down opposite them.

"This here is our meeting room, you might say. All my boarders come here to eat, relax, and talk. Many a time, Olivia and I would sit here and talk."

"What else can you tell us about them?"

"Those two were probably a couple of my best boarders. Always polite, friendly and paid their rent on time. Came to live here about twenty years ago. That would be about the time she must have left North Carolina and her uncle's house. Jessica was just a young girl then. I watched her grow up into a right pretty young woman."

Just then the kettle began to whistle and she jumped up to get it. While the old woman was at the stove, Jonathan looked around the kitchen. It reminded him of so many warm and friendly kitchens of the women of his church. Blue flowered wallpaper covered two of the walls while the rest was painted a light blue. To his mind even though it was all faded, it still looked lovely. Behind him was a door which led to a spacious pantry and he could see many shelves filled with cans and other foods. He imagined that Mrs. Watkins probably did all of her own canning and then shared these with her boarders. The room had quite a few cabinets, all painted an antique white with blue fruit on each one. He felt so at home in this place that he wished he could sit there for hours and talk with this woman. After pouring three cups of coffee, she set them in front of them along with a large tin of chocolate chip cookies.

Sitting down across from them, she resumed her memories. "Yes, Olivia Weston was a very special person to me, especially after my husband passed away. I don't know what I would have done without her. She would sit here for hours just listening to me talk and giving me comfort. Why sometimes I'd feel so low that I couldn't talk and she'd read to me from her Bible or just pray with me. Many a time she would have just got home from the hospital and was dead tired but she always took time. She was a good Christian woman, she was."

"What about Jessica? What was she like?"

"She wasn't anything like her mother -oh, no- not a bit alike at all. Jessica was so quiet and shy - kept to herself mostly. One thing she did have of her mother's was a kind heart. Many a time, she would run errands for me or do little chores around here. Our favorite time was baking cookies and then she would talk to me a might, but not too much. When she became a young woman, she looked so much like her mother, pretty and sweet, it was unbelievable."

Jonathan saw Jack was looking a little impatient listening to the woman reminisce. He started to speak but Jonathan shook his head and he slumped down further in his chair.

Mrs. Watkins had not noticed but kept on talking. "That Olivia sure was a fine Christian lady. All the time she was talking about Jesus and all he had done for her. She being a widow too made me listen to what she said. One night here in the kitchen I asked the Lord to save me and He did. I've been so much happier ever since. The Bible says, `Whosoever shall call upon the name of the Lord shall be saved.' Do you boys know the Lord?"

At her question, Jack could constrain himself no longer and stood up. "This is all very interesting but it doesn't help us find Jessica. Isn't there anything else you could tell that might be of some help? We don't have a whole lot of time, you know." Mrs. Watkins could only sit and stare at Jack for a moment. Turning to Jonathan she said with a smile, "Right impatient young man, isn't He?"

"Yes, Ma'am, I reckon he is. He is right about one thing, though, and that is we don't have much time. Our client could die any time now. But to answer your question, I do know the Lord for about ten years now. Do you know of anyone, perhaps someone in the building, who might tell us where she went?"

"Well, she didn't have too many friends - rather quiet like I told you. The only person who might know something is a teacher who still lives here. They used to talk for hours up in her room about all kinds of things that Jessica learned at school. Her name's Emily Jackson. Would you like to meet her? I think she's home today."

"Yes, please. I am sorry to sound impatient, but I believe you can understand." Jack sounded more polite than previously as he sat back down.

"Don't ya'll worry about it, I reckon I do. I'll just go upstairs and see if she's there. Ya'll just stay put - pour yourself another cup of coffee and please eat some more of those cookies - both of you could use some good cooking from the looks of you." As she admonished them, she left the room.

Jack walked over to the stove and fixed another cup. "I sure do hope this teacher has more information than that old woman. Whew! What a talker! I thought she would never quit. Want another cup, Jonathan?"

"No thanks. She's just a nice old lady who likes to talk. Let's just wait now."

They waited for what seem like a long time and began to wonder if this would be another dead end. However, Mrs. Watkins soon came back with another woman following her. Miss Jackson was a tall, slender woman of about fifty years with a manner that said she was a teacher. Both men stood up as the women entered. The older woman introduced them and had everyone sit down at the table.

Miss Jackson said, "I understand you are trying to locate Jessica Weston. Mrs. Watkins told me the whole story but I am not convinced of your intentions." Her voice seemed full of suspicion and doubt.

"I assure you, Miss Jackson. We only want to find Jessica for her great uncle who wished to see her again before he dies which will probably be soon. Do you know where she is?"

"I do, in a way." She hesitated and looked them over thoroughly before speaking again. "Mrs. Watkins vouches for you and she is a good judge of character, so I guess I can tell you the little bit I know.

"After Jessica's mother died, she really did not know where to turn. We talked for hours and finally she decided to move away from here and all the memories of her mother. Her desire at the time was to go to college. I suggested she try to get into my alma mater, James Madison University."

"I'm not familiar with the school. Where is it?" Jack asked.

"It is in Harrisonburg - over in the Shenendoah Valley. I'm surprised you haven't heard of it."

"Did she take your advice and go there?"

"Yes, she did. I gave her the names of some people I know in the Valley near Harrisonburg whom I said could help her. I could also give you those names if you think it would help. However, I haven't heard from her for several months. I cannot be sure that she is even in that area now."

"That would be most helpful. You really don't have an exact address. Harrisonburg is a large place, I assume."

"One thing might help you a little. Jessica had worked as a waitress here in Richmond so perhaps she would find a restaurant in which to work there. That is about all I can tell you."

"We do appreciate all the help from both of you ladies. Perhaps she will be easy to find there. Thank you so much."

As she wrote down the names and addresses of her friend's in Jonathan's notebook, Miss Jackson commented, "I am sorry I was so distrustful of you at first. However, a few months ago, a man called me on the telephone and demanded information about Jessica. I did not like his attitude at all so I told him nothing and I was afraid you worked with him. You remember that, Mrs. Watkins?"

"Well, yes. Now that you mention it I do. He came here a number of times and I told him I didn't know anything about where Jessica was living or anything, which was the truth. He acted like he didn't believe me though. Pretty soon he just stopped coming. I'm glad to hear that you are not connected with him. He certainly wasn't very nice."

Jonathan looked at his partner to see that he was also shocked to hear that bit of news. So someone else really had been looking for the Westons. Their questions were the same - who was this man and why he was looking for the Westons? Jack was soon able to say, "No, Ma'am. We don't know anything about him except we seem to be following his trail. Perhaps he didn't find her after all."

As they began to leave, Miss Jackson asked them to wait while she went to get something from her room. Soon she came back downstairs and handed them a picture. "I wasn't sure if I could find this picture, but it is one of Jessica that I took just before she left. You may take it if you promise to mail it back to me."

Both men promised that they would take good care of it and mail it back to her as soon as they could get copies. Again they thanked the two women for all their help and Mrs. Watkins for her hospitality. The two women asked them to tell Jessica if they found her to write to each of them.

Back in their motel room, they made plans to leave for Harrisonburg the next day. At least that night they would have more encouraging news to tell Mr. Garland. While Jack studied the road map, Jonathan sat, staring at Jessica's picture. He was convinced she was a most beautiful woman, just as he had hoped. Perhaps she was also a kind, Christian woman like her mother had been. Now he was more anxious than ever to find her.

CHAPTER 14

A cooling breeze stirred the wind chimes in the summer house as Jessica sat and watched the sun fade behind the house. The day had been hot and humid, typical of July days in Virginia. Now she was at ease in the one place on the estate she felt was her own.

The fresh smell of roses trailed into her senses. She remembered how long ago in Richmond her mother had planted her favorite flowers in Mrs. Watkins garden - roses, yellow roses. It had been a hot day like today that her mother and she dug in the ground and put the roses along the fence in front of the house. She wondered if those roses were still blooming like these around her now. Looking at the flowers, she noticed there was a concert of pink and red, but not one, single yellow rose in sight.

"If mother were alive, there'd be yellow roses here. Maybe I could plant some," she murmured out loud. "Oh I do wish mother were here now. She would know what to do."

She still questioned the morning's events in her mind. Why was Adrian so against her visiting his office? He had never explained that to her complete satisfaction. Of course his explanation of the scene with Mrs. Simms was plausible enough for her. He was only trying to help her with her money worries, which was very kind.

Now as the light began to dim, she smiled as she remembered his change of heart over lunch. At the deli, he was the typical newlywed, holding her hand, and whispering how he loved her. Clyde had teased them that now that they were married, they could stop being little love birds. Adrian had only smiled and told him they were planning to act that way for the rest of their lives together. She was so happy with him at the moment that even her questions seemed trivial.

After what seemed to be but a moment, he had to go back to his office. She had offered to walk with him, but he just smiled and said she ought to visit with her friends. To this idea, she readily agreed. Norma Jean had the afternoon off, so they crossed the street to the lawn in front of the courthouse. In the shade of an old, hickory tree, the two women sat on the grass. For a couple of hours, they laughed and talked of old times and shared joys.

Jessica told her friend of the beauty of Hawaii and showed off her snapshots. She spoke of the flowers of every imaginable color and the blue of the ocean and sky. Most of all she related the love she had found with Adrian and her happiness. One thing that pleased Norma Jean was how Jessica appreciated her gift of the Bible and reading it. She told Jessica how she had been praying for her to come back to the Lord. For a moment, Jessica almost told her friend about her doubts of the morning, but just as quickly decided to forget it. There was no need to spoil the happy time they shared. Then they had parted, vowing to get together the next week for lunch. A whip-poor-will calling in the distance brought Jessica back to the present in the gazebo. She noticed a car's lights in front of the house and realized it could only be Adrian. Quickly, she gathered her things and walked back to the house. By the time she reached the front hall, Adrian was already in the library. She could hear him and Mrs. Simms talking, but a third voice she did not recognize made her pause at the door.

"Well, Adrian! Something has got to be done and soon. I can only keep them waiting if I have something to offer." The stranger's voice was urgent and loud.

"Shh - Bill. I don't want my wife to hear us talking about this. So please, keep your voice down." Adrian pleaded in a low voice so that Jessica had to move closer to the door to be able to hear them at all. "Mrs. Simms, do you know where Jessica is?"

"Why, she's sitting out in the gazebo dreaming or something. Don't worry, she won't be in for a while."

"Oh, very well! What are you going to do then?" the stranger called Bill said in a lower and calmer voice.

Adrian seemed calm, yet in control as he spoke again. "Let's just run over what has happened. What have you heard about our holdings in South Africa?"

"As you know, Adrian, we still owe a great deal of money for our diamond mine shares that we bought on margin. With all the unrest there, our creditors want their money quick. If we fail to deliver, they'll just take over control and buy us out at a fraction of the worth of the shares. They'll want an answer and a payment soon."

"We'll just have to borrow some money, that's all. Call the bank tomorrow and use our oil leases in Alaska as collateral. That should get us through another month."

"Wait a minute!" Bill's voice seemed more pleading. "We are almost to the limit of borrowing on the oil leases. Why, if we don't start paying some of those loans back, we could lose that, too."

Adrian's reply was firm and commanding as he said to the man, "Look, Bill, we just have to hold on for a while longer. Any day now that large sum of money will come in and we'll be back on firm ground. We just have to wait. The plans we made are working even now and I won't give up on it just yet. Borrow the money and stall them as best you can. If you have a better solution, we'd like to hear it."

There was silence in the library and Jessica wondered what was happening. Soon, Bill said, "No. I can't think of any other way out of this mess. You've got to realize, Adrian, that we are on the brink of collapse, maybe even bankruptcy. These measures can only be temporary. Can you really be as sure that you'll get all the money and not just part of it? Perhaps something might go wrong and she won't be willing to use the rest of the money on your business."

"Of course he's sure." Mrs. Simms interrupted. "Hasn't he always come through with the needed funds? You'll just have to stop worrying so much and do the job you're paid to do."

"All right. But that money had better get here soon. I don't know how much longer we can stay afloat. Why, we are already a couple months behind on the house payments. If only this place weren't so heavily mortgaged, we could at least sell it. It's worth a fortune on today's market."

"That we cannot do. The money will be here soon. I just can't imagine the old man holding out on us much longer. Don't worry! You'd better leave before my wife comes in, though. Call the bank and we'll discuss this further, tomorrow at the office."

"I'll do what I can, Adrian. But it won't be easy."

"Now you're talking, Bill! I'll show you to the door."

Jessica realized that the two men would be coming out of the library in a moment. She had better not let her husband know she had been listening to their conversation. Looking around, she was able to slip behind the large coat rack in the hall, just before they came out of the room.

From her hiding place, she could see both men clearly. Dressed in a dark gray suit, the stranger named Bill was shorter than Adrian with a build that suggested years of over eating. He walked with a slight limp and she estimated that he must be in his late fifties. He looked worried, which seemed to fit his wrinkled and bearded face.

After he closed the door, Adrian leaned against it for a few moments. His previous look of confidence which he had displayed for Bill had been replaced by a face of worry and fatigue. For a moment, she wanted to run out and comfort him. Perhaps she could give him some words of encouragement or just her love to make him feel better. But she knew how angry he would be if he knew she had been listening, so she stayed behind the coat rack. Soon, he went back into the library.

Long minutes passed while she waited outside the door, wondering what to do. There was silence in the library as she only heard someone pacing back and forth in the room. Finally, she found the courage to peek around the door and into the library. She had not spent much time in this room, for it was usually locked. On the three walls were bookcase which should have been filled with hundreds of books, but to her surprise, were empty. In the middle of the room was a large table with straight back chairs that reminded her of a public library. Over by the far wall were two chairs angled in towards the stone fireplace. Both of them were standing, gazing into the flickering flames. Mrs. Simms had her hand on his shoulder.

"Well now, what do we do? We're going to lose it all if we don't get that money soon. How much longer can he make us wait?"

Mrs. Simms spoke lovingly and reassuring to him, "It will all be over soon, Adrian. You just have to be strong. All your plans are working, so don't give up now. Just remember that."

"You're right." He sat down in one of the wing back chairs. "Would you mind going to find my wife? I'm famished. We need to get dinner soon."

Not waiting for her reply, Jessica silently ran up the stairs to their bedroom. Once inside, she quickly took off her dress and put on her dressing gown to make it look like she had been there all the time. She then sat down at her vanity and began to brush her hair.

A loud rap came at the door, and Jessica turned just as the housekeeper entered. "Mr. Daniels is home and ready for dinner. Will you be long?"

"Oh, Mrs. Simms! I just lost track of time. Tell Adrian I'll be down as soon as I can get dressed. Has he been home long?" Her voice was a little shaky for she was still out of breath from her dash up the stairs. She hoped the housekeeper would only think it was from rushing around the room to get dressed, and not for the true reason.

The housekeeper seemed not to notice and only said, "No, not long. I'll tell him that you will be down in ten minutes. That is when I will begin serving." The woman left, closing the door behind her.

Jessica could only sigh in relief, hoping that she had convinced the other woman that she had been in the bedroom all the time. "I just can't believe he's in so much financial trouble. That's probably why he didn't want me to go to his office today because I might have found out about all of this. Imagine him not wanting to upset me by keeping it to himself like that." She sighed and said, "I wish there was some way I could help him, but I don't have any money. If only I had a rich relative to leave me a fortune. What a laugh!"

She quickly dressed and went down to dinner. As she was walking down the stairs, a thought came to her mind that made her smile. "I'll just have to pray for him and maybe he will tell me about his problems. Perhaps now that these troubles have plagued him, he'll be more open to the Gospel. I'll just have to let him know I love him no matter what happens. But I still wish I had money to help him, for I most certainly would give it to him. Oh, where are your rich relatives when you need them?"

Chapter 15

Jessica's uncle was at that moment beginning another restless night. As he lay in his bed, he was thinking about Olivia and Jessica, hoping they would soon be found. Deep within he felt that his life would soon be over. Earlier, he had asked William not to give him his sedative until the two men had called with the news of their search. While he waited, he removed a legal folder from the desk next to his bed and began to read.

Soon the door opened and William entered carrying a tray. He moved slowly across the room and placed the tray on the night stand next to the bed. On the tray was a pitcher of ice water, a glass, and four bottles of medicine.

"Do I have to take all that? No wonder I'm so sick with all those pills and stuff."

"Yes, Mr. Garland, you do. The doctor gave very specific instructions which I have carried out to the letter. Now if you will allow me to assist you into a sitting position, I will administer your medicine.

"All right, if you must, you must." As Mr. Garland sat up with William's help and a few extra pillows, he reached for the folder lying on the bed beside him. "Let's wait a while on the sedative and I promise I'll take it without a fuss. I need to talk to you about important matters. Please sit down."

At his urging, the butler pulled up a chair next to the bed. "Very well, sir. What is it you wish to discuss?"

The old man asked, "Well, what have we heard from those two boys up there in Virginia? I believe I heard the phone ring a while back. Have they found Olivia and Jessica?"

William cleared his throat and shifted uneasily in his chair. For a few moments, he was unsure of how much he should tell his employer and friend about the report, especially Olivia's death.

Finally he said, "Yes, sir, they called forty-five minutes ago and they have not found them. However, they know that Jessica is now living in Harrisonburg and may be attending school there. They have some contacts there and are going to Harrisonburg first thing in the morning."

Unable to look in the face of the old man, he kept his gaze down at the floor. There was a brief moment of silence as the old man studied his butler and noticed he was uneasy about something as if he was not telling him all of the report.

In a commanding but weak voice, he spoke. "William, you're not telling everything. We have been together too long for me not to be able to tell when you are not honest with me. You never could lie. Don't try to spare my feelings, just recount everything they said to you. After all, that is what I'm paying those boys to do for me. Why aren't they still looking for Olivia? Have they found her?"

"In a manner of speaking they did find her. I was not so sure how to tell you. I suppose that I would have said this in the morning when you are stronger and can take the news..."

"For heaven's sake, tell me, William!"

"All right, sir. It seems Olivia was killed in an automobile accident about two years ago in Richmond. They were able to confirm the information through people who knew both of the women. Also they visited her grave just to be sure. I am really sorry, sir."

The old man turned his face away from the sight of the butler and felt the tears welling up in his eyes. The news had been a great shock to him and it grieved him to realize he would never see his niece again. She was the one who helped him recover and outwit those doctors so many years ago. Now even she could not help him and the situation seemed hopeless.

He remembered how she came into his room with his medicine dressed in jeans and a colorful shirt. He had insisted that she not wear her white uniforms around the house because she was family and it made him feel better not to be reminded he needed a nurse. She would be carrying a tray of medicine. However, she always seemed to be cheerful and made the room seem sunny even on cloudy days. For hours, she talked with him or sat while he rested and read her Bible.

Many times he made fun of her simple beliefs and tried to trick her with hard questions about the book. She told him about the love God showed by sending Jesus to the world to die for man's sins. Her favorite topic was how Jesus had saved her and that she was going to Heaven when she died. She had even tried to get him to trust Jesus but he had always said there was time for that later and besides he did not need any religion. Even in the face of his ridicule and questions, she would smile and say that she would continue to pray for him. He wished he could hear her sweet voice telling him the story again, but now that was impossible. How could she be dead? Was she really in Heaven right now?

For minutes, he sadly thought about Olivia and how he probably would never see her again. A new hope came into his mind. What about Jessica? She was alive. If only she would be willing to come and see him. Turning, he noticed William was still sitting silently in his chair looking out the window.

"Thank you for being honest about Olivia's death. I can't believe she's gone but there is still Jessica to be found. Do you remember her and the pretty smile that brightened this house? I can almost hear her little voice with all her questions. What a joy she was then."

For an hour, the two men talked about the little girl who had lived in their house with her mother so many years ago. She had been quiet unless she had found a topic to ask questions and then she could talk. Her laughter had always brought joy to the household. Mr. Garland especially remembered how she would listen to his old hunting stories and then ask for more. Of course, he could never turn down the opportunity to tell those tales.

"The story she liked best was the one about the dogs. Any story that had to do with my old hounds were her favorites. She spoiled those dogs while she was here. I can still see her sitting by the bed with her eyes so big, completely spellbound by my tale. She was so good for my ego and so friendly. Remember, William?"

William smiled and said, "I sure do, sir. You are right, she was such a happy child. When you were sleeping, she followed me around the house. Funny how my chores seemed more pleasant when she was here. She helped me out in the kitchen mixing batter or getting things for me.

"She liked to hear me tell her of my trips to London as a small lad just to catch a glimpse of the king and queen in all their finery. I told her about waiting near the entrance of the palace as the horse drawn carriage would come out with all the guards in their bright uniforms riding down the street. We would cheer when we got a sight of the royal family. Jessica's eyes would fairly glow as she asked me questions and made me promise to take her there some day. Oh, she loved to listen and I guess I took great pride in relating yarns about my native country to her."

Both men smiled and were silent for a while as they thought of the two women they were trying to find. William looked at his watch and saw that the hour was late. "It is time for you to be getting your rest. We do not want to tire you needlessly. We will get no more information tonight."

"Before you go, there is something I want you know about my will and why I am so desperate to find them."

He reached over and picked up the folder he had been reading earlier. Turning the pages, he found the information and motioned for the butler to be seated.

"Sir, you do not need to confide in me."

"I want to. Please listen carefully. My partner, Mr. Emery will of course handle the reading of the will. Under no circumstances is that old fogy, Mr. Mason, to have anything to do with. Do you understand?"

"Isn't he the partner who handled your wife's side of the divorce?"

"Yes, he is. Now I have left you a sizable pension that will be quite adequate if you wish to retire and maybe go back to England and be that country gentleman you've always wanted to be. Will this be enough, you think?"

Holding the papers in front of Williams' face, he pointed to an amount highlighted on the page. The butler's mouth dropped as he read the amount. It certainly was a lot of money.

"Why, sir, that is a fortune. I would really live like a gentleman on that money. But it is far too generous. I do not deserve it, but I thank you. What can I say?"

"Your thanks is sufficient, for you do deserve every penny of it for all the years you've put up with me. I reckon you wonder about the rest of the estate."

"It really is none of my business but..."

"Don't give me that. I know you're curious and I want to tell someone just in case I die before they can find Jessica. I have decided to leave about one-third of my estate to my worthless son and his mother who laughingly called herself my wife years ago. I just couldn't write them out completely but I sure thought about it. She got too much of my money at the settlement. Did I ever tell you about that?"

William shook his head. "Only a little bit, sir. You never wanted to talk about it before now."

"You are right about that and I don't rightly want to now but I must. That sure was a shock to me. She said I wasn't much of a husband or father even though she felt no guilt about spending my money. I reckon no woman spent money faster than her but I never denied her or the boy anything. She said I cared more about my law practice than her. How did she think I could afford her spending habits except to work a lot?"

"Anyhow, after a few years of all that jabbering and nagging, I agreed to a divorce. Why, she even had some other fellow willing to marry her and be around more than me. Some wimp who couldn't wait to get his hands on some of my money as well as my son. She went out and hired Mr. Mason to take her case to court and it was soon over. I didn't have the desire to fight it. So good riddance."

"He wasn't in your law firm then, was he?"

"That's right. At the time he had his own law practice over in Winston-Salem. He got her a big settlement, too much if you ask me and I'm still paying. Then she took off and married that other fellow and moved away to somewhere in Virginia. I forget that man's name right now but he adopted my son and that boy has got his name not mine. She's poisoned my son's mind against me by this time, I reckon."

He paused to take a sip of water and then continued his narrative. "Then a few years later, Mason wanted to join our law firm as a partner. My other partners thought it would add a lot of wealthy clients and double the size of our practice. I was against it all along but I let myself get talked into it with the condition that he would stay out of my way at the office. I hardly ever saw him there. I still regret that decision."

"If that is all..."

"No, it is not all. I wanted to leave the rest of my estate to Olivia and Jessica. That is why I hired Jonathan and Jack to find them because I wished to tell them the good news myself. She was the only relative who showed any kindness to me without regard to my money. Now that Olivia is passed away, it should go to her daughter."

"But, sir, won't your wife and son contest the will?"

"Oh, I'm sure they will but Phillip Emery is a good lawyer and he'll do right by me. That is why I only want him to read the will. I just couldn't leave all my money to two people who don't care about me. Neither of them have bothered to come and see me in all the years since the divorce. They have not bothered to write or let me know anything about my son. Every letter or card that I sent to them has been returned unopened. I know that Olivia and Jessica cared about me. Besides it is my money and I can leave it to whomever I want. Do you agree?"

"Yes, of course, I agree. Your wife and son had moved out when I came to work for you. Quite frankly, sir, I do not remember much about them at all. But would you wish me to contact them about your condition? Surely they would want to visit you now?"

At those words, he sat up in bed and said, "No, William! Your are not to contact them at all. Let the lawyers contact them after I'm gone. I don't want to see them and I reckon they don't really want to see me either. Besides, I'm tired. Please give me my medicine so I can get some sleep. Oh, and put these papers back in my desk."

William took the papers from the old man and returned them to the nearby desk. As he gave him the medicine, he said to his employer, "I hope they can find Jessica. It would do us both good to see her again. She has probably become a fine young woman by now."

Turning out the lights, the butler left the room. In the hall, he stood in front of the door for a moment. He tried to pray for a quick and successful end for the search. That old man was not just his employer but had become his best friend. It hurt to see him suffer so much grief now.

Out loud, he whispered, "Just find her, please, just find her." Turning out the lights, he went down the stairs to lock up and retire for the night.

CHAPTER 16

Days later, Jonathan and Jack felt they had visited every restaurant in Harrisonburg and the surrounding county. At each stop, they had showed the picture of Jessica to the people there. No one could recall the young woman working at their restaurant or even having been there. Now they began to wonder whether she had ever come to that city.

They had visited the people whom she should have contacted on her arrival there. All but one of the families had moved away but the last family on the list was still in the area. Arriving at the address in the telephone directory, the house was a large brick ranch with a small yard in a quiet neighborhood. The wife was at home and she agreed to answer their questions. She was a middle aged woman, tall and slender with dark hair and features. Her clothes were a casual pair of jeans and a sweater.

While seated at the table in a rather small kitchen, she said, "Why, yes, I reckon I do remember Emily Jackson sending me a letter several months ago about a young woman coming to the area. Emily is a friend from my college days and we were anxious to help her young friend in any way we could. Since the girl had no family to speak of, we..."

"When did she contact you?"

"That is the strange part about it all. I am afraid that we never heard from her. I had forgotten about it until now."

"Are you sure she never contacted you? Miss Jackson was so sure about her coming here."

Jonathan tried to hide the disappointment in his voice but he realized here was another dead end to the trail. This was too hard to believe.

"I am quite sure. I had intended to write Emily to let her know about the girl but it must have slipped my mind. I'm sorry I can't help you. If you leave a number where I can reach you, I'll let you know if I hear from her. You know though that if she hasn't called me by now she probably won't."

Realizing that the lady could not be of any further help, Jack gave her the telephone number at the motel, and they left the house. Both of them were sure that if Jessica had not called on the family by this time, she certainly would not now.

Now as they sat on the steps of the courthouse, Jack spoke, "Well, I guess we better get some lunch and try another restaurant. Look there's a deli across the street. Let's go check it out."

Jonathan looked up at the place Jack mentioned and his first thought was, `Why bother?'. The deli seemed so small and run down from where he was sitting that he wanted to go elsewhere. Jack had not waited for his answer, but was already walking down the steps towards the shop. Shrugging his shoulders, he followed his partner's lead.

Inside the shop, Jonathan was surprised at the appearance which contrasted with the forgotten look of the outside of the building. It had reminded him on so many places in the downtown area after most of the businesses had moved to the new shopping malls outside the city limits. The inside was clean and modern. The tables and booths were covered with bright red and white checked tablecloths with napkin holders shaped like flowers. On the walls were pictures of the surrounding area. At the far end of the shop, a counter like the ones from old soda shops stretched across the whole back wall. Every chair seemed to be taken until he noticed Jack sitting at the counter by an empty stool. Jack was already reading a menu when he glanced up and motioned for Jonathan to sit down next to him.

As he sat down, a waitress with a pleasant smile approached and said, "Howdy, boys! Y'all are new to Clyde's aren't you? Here's a menu."

For a moment, Jonathan stared into the face of the smiling waitress. He sensed a joy in her voice and smile. She was a friendly looking woman of middle age about five foot one or two inches. Her hair was dark but sprinkled with touches of gray and combed neatly into a bun held up by a large, tortoise colored hair-clip. This gave her a look of beauty which came from her smile. He felt at once comfortable to be talking to this woman even though she was a stranger to him.

Jack closed the menu, "We'll have two of your luncheon specials and hopefully some information."

"Well, I know I can get you fellows the specials but I'm not so sure of the other. What kind of information do you want?"

"We're looking for a young woman for a client of ours. He's her relative and is quite anxious to find her. We have good reason to believe that she moved to the area a couple years ago and is probably working in a restaurant. We've shown her picture all over this city with no luck so far. Would you mind looking at her picture and telling us if you've ever seen her?" Handing the photograph to the waitress, he waited for the usual shake of the head and denial of ever seeing the girl.

She wiped her hands on her red and white apron and took the picture. Jonathan held his breath and said a silent prayer that at last they had found a person who knew Jessica. They were allowed only a moment of suspense for as soon as she looked at it, her face lit up in a bigger grin and she said, "Why, I sure do know her! That's Jessica, my best friend."

"Praise the Lord!" Jonathan said aloud so that several of the customers looked his way. "You don't know how happy that bit of news makes us. We were just about ready to give up. Is she here now? How can we get in touch with her?"

Norma Jean leaned over the counter and whispered to them, "Look fellows, I can't talk too much now. As you see, we're right busy and my boss won't like it if I ignore the rest of my customers and talk to you." She had noticed Clyde looking her way from the other end of the counter. "My name's Norma Jean. Why don't ya'll wait for me until the lunch rush is over, then I'll take a break and we can talk. Okay? I'll get your lunch."

"Hey, things are finally starting to fall into place." Jack slapped him on the back with a big grin on his face. "I feel so good I could eat a horse. How about you? I sure do hope the food is edible."

Jonathan only smiled as Norma Jean brought their orders of two hot dogs with chili, potato salad, and cole slaw and returned to serving the other people at the counter. "I hope I don't get a case of heartburn from eating this. Why didn't you tell me this was the luncheon special? I'm sure I would have ordered something a little better."

"For one thing you didn't ask me and for another I was too busy trying to show the picture to really read the menu. Go ahead and eat it! It's not so bad." Jack began to eat as if this was the first food placed in front of him in several days. Not wishing to appear ungracious, Jonathan also began eating and hoped that their search would soon be over so he could give up eating in these restaurants. It seemed like Jack was always ordering junk food for him and he was getting tired of it.

The rest of the meal was eaten in silence as both men kept their eyes on the waitress for they did not want her to get away from them. Now they felt like their search would finally come to an end. The wait seemed long and they lingered over their cups of coffee waiting for Norma Jean's break. As she served the other people at the counter, she would look at them, smile and say, "Won't be too long. Want something else?"

Jonathan had other thoughts which were foreign to Jack. He was anxious to end the search, for in the days since he had taken the job of finding her, he had wanted to find her for his own sake. There was something about her face that was constantly in his mind and even in his sleep. Often he wondered if it were possible to fall in love with someone just from a photograph and other people's memories.

One thing he hoped for more than anything else was that she would be a Christian. Perhaps she had developed a character like her mother- loving, warm, and living for Jesus. His fantasies saw her that way and her eventually caring for him in the same way that he might come to care for her. He found himself only half listening to Jack's conversation and watching the door, just in case Jessica might walk into the shop.

As they waited, the lunch crowd began to thin and soon they were the only ones left. Norma Jean came out from behind the counter and motioned them over to a table on the far side of the room. Once they were all seated, she said, "Could you let me see the picture again so I can be sure it is Jessica? Then you can tell me who you are and why you need to find her."

Jonathan handed her the picture and said, "My name's Jonathan Miner and this is Jack Sampson. I'm a lawyer and he's a private investigator. Our client, Mr. Thomas Garland is Jessica Weston's uncle who wishes to locate her. We need to find her quickly because he is dying and wants to see her again."

"Well then! You've come to the right place. Jessica worked here and we've become good friends. I just wanted to be careful before I told you too much. A lot of folks say I talk too much as it is.

"But anyhow she doesn't work here now. She got married a few weeks ago to a fellow named Adrian Daniels. He's got a lot of money, so she didn't need this job anymore and quit. She lives over on an estate just east of here next to the Massanutten Mountain. I could give you the phone number."

At the news that Jessica was married, Jonathan felt disappointed and sad. Jack, seeing his partner become silent, spoke up. "That would be great. I could give her a call right now and set up an appointment to meet her." Taking the number that Norma Jean wrote down, he rushed over to the pay phone and began to dial. Jonathan continued to look at the floor and wished that what he had heard was not true.

Norma Jean noticed his sad look and tried to converse with him. "Hey, don't look so sad. You've found her! You should be happy."

"You're right about that." Jonathan replied as he finally looked up.

Just then Jack came back to the table and slapped him on the back. "Hey things are looking up! I just talked to Mr. Daniels and he gave me directions out to their place. He said we could come out anytime this afternoon. We've finally found her. Mr. Garland will be so pleased. I can't wait to tell him!"

Norma Jean looked at the two men and was puzzled at their different reactions. Both of them had been so excited first but now one had become silent at the information she had given. She sat quietly and waited until the two men had made their plans for going to Jessica's house.

"Well now. I was wondering about something." She paused as she waited for them to look in her direction. "I was wondering if you fellows are Christians or not."

Jonathan quickly smiled and nodded his head and said, "Oh yes, I am! I thought you might be." Jack only silently shook his head with a face like a young boy who had been asked if he liked spinach.

"Good. Now I've got the afternoon off and I'd like to go with you to see Jessica. That is, if you don't mind."

"Of course not. We'd love the company and you can tell us more as we drive out."

The three left the deli and were soon driving east on Route 33. Norma Jean told them as much as she could about Jessica and her husband. Jonathan kept asking most of his questions about her husband. From her answers, he got the impression that she did not trust this man who had married Jessica. She gave no specifics except her feelings that the marriage was hasty and ill advised.

Turning the conversation to spiritual things, Jonathan was happy to hear that Jessica was also a Christian. So involved were they in their discussion that they were suddenly aware of the car stopping in front of a large house.

A rather large woman opened the door and introduced herself as the housekeeper at the door. She ushered them into a small drawing room and announced them to a young couple. Immediately they knew that this was indeed Jessica and their search was finally over.

Chapter 17

The plane was now twenty minutes late leaving and Jessica had begun her third cup of coffee. She stirred the hot drink over and over while she stared out the window. Adrian and that other man were busy talking about legal matters, wills and inheritance laws. To her it was all so boring.

Ever since those two men had entered her house yesterday, so much had changed. Now she was on her way back to North Carolina to see her uncle. She was surprised that Adrian was so anxious for her to go. He had practically ordered her to go when she had seemed reluctant. Why did he want her to go? He did not know the old man, and it was unlike him to be concerned about a stranger.

"Flight 701 is now ready for boarding at Gate 2," said a voice over the loudspeaker.

Jonathan was looking at her with a smile and saying, "Come on, Mrs. Daniels, they're calling our flight."

"Yes, darling, you certainly don't want to miss your plane."

Adrian was helping her out of her chair. In fact, she felt more like he was dragging her out of it. Catching her breath, she pulled slightly away from him.

"All right, Adrian! I can get up by myself. Thank you. That is only the first call so the flight won't leave right away. You act as if you are trying to get rid of me." She tried to put a cold touch to her voice to make him feel bad about not going with her. "Why can't you come? I really don't want to go without you."

"We don't need to go over that again, do we? If I leave that fool of an office manager alone this time he might ruin me. I had an awful mess to clean up when I returned from our honeymoon. Please dear, I thought you understood."

His face was red and he turned away from her gaze. "Come now, Jonathan is waiting for you at the gate. I really must get back to work. After all, I'm giving up my lunch hour to see you off."

"Of course, we wouldn't want you to be late. I'm only leaving for a short time. Will you miss me?"

She grabbed him by his shoulders and pulled him towards her, kissing him as hard as she could. He held her in his arms and returned her kiss as he had once done on their honeymoon, so warm and passionate. If only this moment would last and she could stay with him. It was over all too quickly as a voice entered into this paradise of her mind.

"Excuse me. We have to hurry if we want to get aboard. They just made the final call to board."

Jonathan seemed to her to be a little too impatient to get her aboard the plane. Didn't he know that she needed these last moments with her husband? She would not see for days.

"Sorry, Jonathan." Adrian stepped back and wiped his mouth on his handkerchief. "Ha-ha, can't to back to the office with lipstick all over my face. What would everyone think? You better go, darling."

"Oh, who cares! Tell me good-bye again, Adrian. I'm sure Jonathan can go on board by himself. I'll catch up."

"No, Jessica, you run along. Here, Jonathan, you better help her on the plane. She can be a little slow. Good-bye and have a nice flight. Call me tonight! I've got to go now."

Adrian walked out the waiting area without another word and only turned once to wave before running out the door. She wanted to run after him but Jonathan took her arm and pulled her gently but steadily toward the gate.

Before she had passed through the gate, she noticed a man who left the magazine rack and ran out right behind her husband. It seemed like he was following him. She wondered just who that was and why he looked sort of familiar. By this time, Jonathan had her through the door and she gave up her speculations.

Once on board the airplane, they took their seats in the first class section. Jonathan indicated for her to take the window seat and she readily agreed. This was only her second time on an airplane for her first flight had been with Adrian when they had gone to Hawaii. She still felt nervous as she buckled her seat belt and listened to the safety instructions from the flight attendant. Now all she had to do was wait for the plane to take off. Not wishing to speak to her travel companion, she stared out the window.

Jonathan noticed her nervousness and said, "Is this your first flight?"

"No, it isn't. I've flown a number of times now."

He did not seem to notice the cool tone of her voice as she had not wanted to talk to him yet. He went on, "Well, you did look a bit uneasy but I guess I was mistaken. I don't mind telling you. I still get a little bit of butterflies in my stomach no matter how many flights I take."

She turned to look at him really for the first time since he had met them at the airport. Her only thoughts had been about Adrian and being separated from him. Now she wished that she had not spoken so sharply to him. It was not his fault that Adrian had not chosen to come with her. She might as well make the best of it and enjoy the trip to North Carolina. It would be good to see her uncle again.

Looking at her companion, she was impressed with his smile that seemed to light up his face. It was a handsome and kindly face to which she felt an immediate attraction. He looked too young to be a lawyer. The jeans and turtleneck he wore reminded her more of an athlete than a lawyer.

"I'm sorry that I spoke so harshly to you a moment ago. I guess I am a little nervous after all."

"Don't worry about it. I figured perhaps you might be missing your husband. It was a shame he wasn't able to come along with us. Why don't we pray now and put our minds at ease and our lives in the hands of Jesus."

He placed his hand on hers, bowed his head and began to pray. Jessica quickly bowed her head and listened to him praying for a safe trip and the health of her uncle. She was impressed by his words so simple and honest. Why, he must be a Christian, too. When he said "amen", she looked at him and smiled.

"Thank you for praying, Jonathan. I feel a whole lot better now. I wondered if you were a Christian. I am also. You see, I asked the Lord Jesus into my heart years ago."

"That's wonderful news. I've been a Christian only about five years. I was hoping you were a Christian ever since we started looking for you."

Her reply was to look at him and smile. At that moment, she seemed to be the most beautiful woman he had met. Once again, he wished that she had waited before marrying Adrian. There was nothing left but to sit and at least enjoy the flight down to North Carolina.

The rest of the flight was spent in conversation about the Bible and their lives. Jessica told him about her mother and her life since her mother had died. She even told him about the odd things that her husband had been doing. For one thing, he would not allow her anywhere near his office or to meet any of his co-workers. Even stranger was the night she had overheard his conversation with that odd man. He seemed to be on the brink of bankruptcy but he always spoke to her as if all their finances were solid. In fact, he had been quite insistent that they both sign a will. Wouldn't that show their finances to be in order?

She felt so comfortable with Jonathan that she told him about the mysterious woman client. That scene in front of the deli and his explanation was rather suspicious. Then there were the telephone calls at all hours and his insistence that only the servants answer them. After all, he had said that was part of their job. All of these seemed strange, but she was sure that her husband loved her. Maybe after they had been married longer, he would confide in her more.

Jonathan seemed so understanding. He was willing to listen and not judge Adrian or her. She began to feel he was a trusted friend and could be told anything in confidence. After all, he was her brother in the Lord and a part of the family of God just like she was.

Jonathan felt like he had known her for years instead of only for a few hours. She was so much like the woman he imagined himself marrying that he was comfortable and able to talk to her without any fear. One thing he did not want to tell her was the reason Jack had remained behind in Harrisonburg. He had not trusted her husband the moment they had met. Now he was sure his suspicion was correct. From what she had told him, he had acted very strangely indeed. Their plan was for Jack to follow Adrian and uncover what he was hiding.

However, the more he thought about it, he was not sure if the revelation would be good for her. Perhaps, his feelings of jealousy had made him suspicious of Adrian. Did he really love a woman he had only just met? Sure she was lovely and friendly. Their spirits were drawn together by God's Spirit in their lives. This meant they were only to be good friends.

As they were landing in Hickory, he prayed silently and asked for wisdom. Now he knew that God's will would be done. He would just have to wait to see what Jack discovered and then whatever happens to accept it. For now, he hoped that Jessica would not be hurt too much in the process.

Chapter 18

As they drove through the streets of Hickory, Jessica was surprised at all she remembered. Some of the buildings and streets were still familiar to her even after all the years had passed. When they turned into the street on which her uncle lived, she could barely hide her excitement. The house was just as she remembered it.

It had been many years since she and her mother had stepped out of a taxi in front of the house. She had been frightened to be moving into a new place. What would her uncle be like? Her father had only been dead a few years then and her future seemed so uncertain. They had sold their home and her mother had gone back to work as a live-in nurse. Now she was moving into that big house to take care of an old uncle whom she had never met.

At the door, they had been greeted by a man who had talked strangely. Later her mother told her the man, the butler, was from England and that was how they talked. It did not take her long to feel comfortable with her new surroundings. The big house and the large yard around it gave her plenty of opportunities for play. Soon she had made good friends with the two men in the house. Her uncle was always glad to see her and tell her stories of hunting and exotic animals.

The butler allowed her to follow him around the house and help him with various chores. She still recalled some of his tales of English kings, queens and castles. Whatever else happened, those times were some of the happiest years of her life.

Now Jonathan was helping her out of the car in front of the same house and everything seemed to be the same. What would her uncle be like now? It was hard to believe it was so many years later and she was feeling the same misgivings she had felt the first time she approached this house. Just at that moment, the door was opened and there stood William, the butler, just like the first time. However, this time he wore a big smile and rushed forward to take her hand.

"Oh, Miss Jessica, it is so good to see you again. You look just like your mother did when you two first came here. I'm so sorry to hear of her passing."

"Thank you, William. It's been so long. You haven't changed and this house is still the same as I remembered. How is my uncle today?"

"Now, Miss Jessica, you should not flatter me so. As you can plainly see, I am much older and fatter. Anyhow, Mr. Garland is resting now. I am afraid he had a rather rough time last night. The doctor is concerned he is failing fast. Let's not stand out here in the doorway. Come in! I have a fresh pot of tea in the kitchen with some freshly baked scones to go with it. We can talk there."

Ushering them inside, he led the way back to the kitchen. They made some small talk about the weather and their trip while William poured their tea and put the scones and butter on the table. The kitchen was clean and well organized just as she remembered it. There had been other times when she, her mother and the butler had enjoyed tea at that very table.

The butler sat down and said, "It is so good to have company for tea. Usually, I spend this time alone while Mr. Garland is resting."

"When may I see my uncle, William?"

"Well, now miss, the doctor left strict instructions that he was not to be disturbed until after supper. So I had planned to have supper down here. Then after he has eaten, you may visit him for a short period. Tomorrow he may feel up to a longer visit."

"Yes, that's fine. I'm just anxious to see him. I could use some rest myself after the plane ride. May I go up to my room now?"

"Of course, Miss Jessica. I will show you to your room and perhaps Jonathan will bring your luggage. Supper will be served at six o'clock so you have some hours to yourself. Feel free to make yourself at home. I will be in the kitchen and after you have rested, you may wish to visit with me for a while as I prepare supper."

The butler led the way up the staircase in the hall. The dark mahogany steps and the rich, dark green carpet reminded her of the times she had slid down the banister into the waiting arms of the man walking in front of her. It had been their little game on rainy days. He even thanked her for dusting the railing for him. They climbed to the third floor and turned right down the long hallway. The green carpet and the wallpaper with green ivy was familiar to her. At the last room on the hall, he stopped and opened the door for her to enter.

"Here's your old room, Miss Jessica. I hope you will be comfortable here. We haven't changed much as you can see."

She smiled in amazement because it was so much as she remembered except that the walls seemed to be freshly painted. The light rose color had been her favorite. The four poster bed with the canopy was still on the far side of the room and the little night stand and the lamp with the Tiffany shade was just as she remembered them. Pink, lace curtains were blowing at the open window. All the furnishings were in pink or rose shades.

"William, you kept it just like I had been here yesterday and you have the same colors. It looks so good."

"Mr. Garland wanted your room to look just like you left it when you came back. He was so sure you would. We also kept your mother's room next door the same. Anyhow, I was sure you would want to stay in this room again."

"Thank you that was very kind of you both."

"Rest up now and come down whenever you are ready. We can talk more then."

At that moment, Jonathan set the bags down next to the bed. "I guess that is my cue to leave."

"Why, Jonathan, you've been so quiet, I'd almost forgotten you were here. Will you be here for supper?"

"I'd love to. Is that all right with you William?"

"Of course, you are always welcome. I assume you will need to speak with Mr. Garland then."

"Yes, I will. He'd have my head if I didn't. I just hope he is up to hearing my report. We'd better go downstairs and let Jessica get some rest. See you later."

"Quite right." The two men left Jessica standing alone in the middle of the room. After they closed the door, she went over to the window and looked out on the back yard where she had played so many years ago. The old willow tree that she had swung by its branches was still there. Even the old gazebo at the back was glistening with a new coat of paint. She remembered having so much fun there.

Right next to the window was a rocking chair where her mother had always sat when she was in her room. She recalled how she had sat on her lap as she read the Bible. They did that every night before going to bed. There were many good memories in that room. Suddenly she felt tired and soon, she was fast asleep on the bed.

Back downstairs, the two men went into the kitchen and poured themselves another cup of tea. Sitting down at the table, Jonathan asked, "Do you think Mr. Garland will feel up to hearing my report and a visit from Jessica tonight?"

"I don't know. We are going on day by day and sometimes even hour by hour with him. The doctor appears to be quite pessimistic in his prognosis. Each day I wonder if it will be the last day we have him with us."

"It's that bad? Maybe Jessica's visit will have a good effect on him. Anyhow, I need to wait to hear from Jack. He said he'd call as soon as he knew something. I'll take my bags up to my room after we've talked."

"Fine, your room is ready for you. I thought you might stay here until this is finished. You never did say why Jack did not come back with you. I know you don't have to tell me but..."

"You have every right to know. In fact, it might help if I run it past you before I tell Mr. Garland."

"Of course, I want to help out in anyway I can. I'll just be fixing supper while we talk. It will help pass the time until Jack calls."

For the next hour, Jonathan talked while the butler cut up vegetables for a salad. He told him about their search and how there had always been someone else one step ahead of them looking for the two women. When they finally found Jessica, she had only recently married. He related how he had been uneasy about her husband, Adrian Daniels, and the quick marriage. That was why Jack stayed behind in Harrisonburg. Now they had to wait for the call and they were both sure it would be bad news.

All too soon, the ringing telephone startled them. William answered it and gave the receiver to Jonathan. It was Jack. William watched as the younger man listened and wrote down occasional notes. It was a long conversation but he could tell that they had been right about the bad news.

"After he hung up the telephone, Jonathan turned to the butler and said, "It is worse than I expected."

Chapter 19

Jack had not been idle since Jonathan and Jessica had gone to North Carolina. As soon as Adrian left his house that afternoon, he was right behind him. He had agreed with his partner that something was wrong with this man. Both men were suspicious of him from the first meeting. He followed him to a townhouse on the north side of town. He went inside and Jack settled down to wait.

At first, he was not so sure that it was important to check out Adrian. They had been hired to find Jessica, and they had already accomplished that task. Mr. Garland had not sent them to do anything else. However, what he had found out that morning convinced him to continue to follow Adrian. He was sure his employer would want to help his niece in any way possible.

His first stop was to check out the investment and brokerage firms in Harrisonburg to find out where Adrian worked. Fortunately, there were only a few companies in town. At each place he got the same answer, no one had ever heard of a man named Adrian Daniels.

At one small firm near the end of the list, he got a positive answer. When he asked the receptionist, she said Adrian had been employed there, she asked Jack to wait. Her supervisor could give him more of the information he needed.

After a few minutes, she showed him to another office. Rising to meet him was an attractive woman of around forty years. She was dressed smartly in a light blue suit and her dark hair was pulled back in a ponytail. He was surprised to notice that she was as tall as he and athletically built. She looked more like a professional tennis player than an investment broker. Taking off her glasses, she shook his hand with a firm grip and motioned him to sit down. Her look seemed grim as if she had only bad news to give. He handed her his business card and sat in a chair in front of her desk.

She spoke first after quickly looking at his card. "All right, Mr. Sampson, I see you are a private investigator by your card. I am Mary Wickers, a partner in this firm. I understand from the receptionist you are asking about Adrian Daniels. What is your interest in him?"

"I have been hired by my client, whom I will not name because of client privilege, in North Carolina to find his missing relatives, his niece and her daughter. He is dying, and he wants to see them again. We have found that the niece is deceased but we were able to trace the daughter here to Harrisonburg."

"Please go on."

"It seems the daughter has married Adrian Daniels."

"What does this have to do with Mr. Daniels or this firm? If you have found her, why are checking up on her husband? That doesn't seem to be part of your job."

"You're right in a way but my client is very concerned about her welfare. He has made her his principle heir of a considerable amount. Her marriage being a recent one and also a very hasty one, I wanted to be able to reassure my client. Personally, there just seemed to be something wrong about the guy that I can't really describe. If he is employed here then he checks out all right on that point."

"I did not say he was employed here. I'm afraid your feelings about this man do have some merit. If the young woman he has married is coming into some wealth, and he knows about it, I would be very worried about her welfare indeed."

"Your receptionist said he worked here."

"That is correct, he was an employee here until about a year ago. We found his job performance was unsatisfactory and we fired him."

"Well, that's not what he told his wife. It seems he has led her to believe he was a partner in a brokerage firm and was pulling in a six figure salary."

At this revelation, the woman looked away and out the window behind her desk. After a few moments of silence, she turned back around and slammed her fist down on the desk. Jack was startled by her reaction and he jumped in his seat. Her voice showed that she was angry about something.

"Now, Mr. Sampson, I do not make it a practice to gossip about my employees, current or former. However, this situation sounds dangerous to me. I am afraid that she has married Mr. Daniels under false pretences. I will make an exception in this case."

"You see, Mr. Daniels was not fired simply because of his job performance, which was average at best. Perhaps that could have been worked out as he got more training. We found he had made unauthorized and personal use of our fax machine to send wires to South Africa and Alaska. Also he purchased stocks for himself and others by undercutting prices and using other unethical means. We had to fire him then. Your client may be even more shocked by his personal behavior."

"What do you mean?"

"He was quite a flirt with the young ladies in the office and made some improper advances to them. When he began to go after some of our woman clients, making passes and lewd remarks, this was the last straw. Unless he has changed drastically, that young woman is in store for a great deal of heart break."

"Was there anyone in particular he was coming on to?"

"Why don't I let you look at his personnel file. I had my secretary pull it out before you came in. At first, I was not sure how or if I could help but I believe now that I should cooperate in anyway I can. I do not want him to ruin any more lives. There are a lot of statements from our female employees and clients about his conduct. You may feel free to interview them."

Jack glanced over the papers in the file folder. Even though he had been in the investigation business for a while, some of the statements shocked him. Mr. Garland would not be pleased that this man had married his niece. This man was a womanizer of the worst kind as well as being dishonest in business.

After a few moments, he said, "I bet all this took the wind out of his sails."

"Perhaps not. That man has a lot of gall. Another partner, a man, confronted him and told him he was fired and showed him these documents. Would you believe he laughed? He said he really didn't need this job anymore. I won't repeat any of the language he used."

"Did he say anything else - like he had another job or something?"

"No, It was not that. He mentioned he would be coming into a lot of money as soon as an old man died. Then he just snapped his fingers and left. We have not seen him since. As far as getting another job, I have not received any requests for recommendations from any companies. All of those requests cross my desk for review and I sure would remember his name. You better believe he would never get anything good out of this office."

"He didn't say who the old man was, did he?"

"Well, no. Do you suppose he found out somehow his wife was coming into money? If he did, I believe she is in great danger."

"I had also thought of that. This situation is worse than my partner and I suspected. May I borrow this folder and check up on some of these leads?"

"I really cannot allow the folder to leave the office. However, we do want to help you in any way we can. My secretary can help you by copying any of the material in the folder. If you wish to speak to any of the women involved, she can call them and see if they are willing to speak to you. I would like to help you more but I have a very important meeting if fifteen minutes."

"You have been most helpful. My suspicions seem to be correct and my client's niece will need help."

"I do not need to tell you this but please be careful yourself. I do not trust that man at all. Just between you and me, I hope you can nail him for something before he causes more trouble or hurts the young woman."

"Yes, I hope we are not too late."

"Please leave a number where you can be reached with my secretary and if I think of anything else, I will be sure to call you."

Thanking her, Jack got up and left her office. True to her word, the secretary and he made a number of copies. She was also able to introduce him to a number of the women employees who were quite willing to tell him about Adrian. None of them had anything good to say and they all were worried that he had fooled someone into marrying him. If he needed any of them to testify in court against him, they were all willing. He even talked over the telephone to some of the firm's female clients and they told him the same story. Now he had some hard evidence on Mr. Daniels.

Leaving the telephone number of the motel where he was staying with the secretary, he left.

Soon Adrian came out of the townhouse and Jack pulled his car behind him. He drove to several stores before going back to his house. Feeling this was not going to produce anything, Jack went back to his motel room.

Later that day, he called down to Mr. Garland's house to tell Jonathan just what he had found out. "Well, I hate to admit it but it looks like our suspicions are somewhat correct. He does not have a job like he told Jessica."

"You're right, Jack, but the other allegations bother me a whole lot more. What other things has he lied about? What will you do tomorrow?"

"It is going to get a lot worse. I'm going to keep tailing him. He's got to slip up somewhere. If he propositioned so many women, there has to be one he was successful with. I'll find out."

"Any leads?"

"Right now, he has been going to this townhouse on the north side of town. I'm going to stake it out until it yields some results. It is just not going to be good."

"You're right. How are we going to tell Jessica? It will break her heart if he is cheating on her."

"Look, you only just met her. You talk like she's your long lost sister or girlfriend or something. Hey, you've got to keep it all in perspective and professional. You better tell Mr. Garland what I've found out. Call me back right after you talk to him and let me know if I should pursue this investigation of Adrian any further. I'd really like to nail that guy."

"Sure thing, Jack. Anything else you need?"

"Yeah, I'm running a little low on money. See if he will advance some money into my account. Keep your fingers crossed."

Jonathan hung up the telephone and went up to see his employer, Mr. Garland. At the door, he met William who had just come out of the old man's room. He was shown into the room and spent a difficult half hour as he explained carefully just what Jack had learned. Knowing the nature of the old man's illness, he tried to break the news slowly. Even with that in mind, he could tell that he was getting upset. It did not take any persuasion to get permission to continue the investigation and send more money to Jack.

After leaving the room, he went straight back to the telephone and called Jack.

"You've got the go ahead, and I'll be putting another five hundred dollars into your account this morning. The old man said to let him know when you will need more money. And be absolutely sure of all your findings. This could be tricky."

"Did he say anything else?"

"Yeah, it was kind of funny at first. When I told him the name of Adrian, he sat up real straight in the bed. He said he was thinking of someone else with that name but that is all he would tell me. That was right before he said for you to be very careful and get a lot of supporting evidence."

"You're right that was odd. Anyhow, I have a lot of leads to track down. I'm going to need some help. Can you come back up here?"

"No, afraid not. Mr. Garland has me taking care of his will and such. Maybe you could get Jessica's friend, Norma Jean to help you. She seems pretty smart to me and I'm sure she'll be willing to help."

"Good thinking. I'll go there for lunch tomorrow and see if she can get any time off. Thanks for the advice and the money. Call you tomorrow."

The next day, Jack went to the townhouse early and parked where he was able to see the front door. He had a thermos of coffee and a dozen doughnuts to help the long wait. He had only drunk one cup and eaten two doughnuts when Adrian's car pulled up in front of the townhouse. He got out and went inside.

Only a few moments later, a red Pontiac Firebird convertible parked next to his car. Out of it jumped a lovely red headed woman. She was about five foot four and was wearing blue shorts and a black tank top. From where he was watching he was very impressed with her looks. She ran up to the door and into the arms of Adrian Daniels who had come out onto the front porch. Quickly, he pulled her inside, looked up and down the street and slammed the door.

"What a scene!" Jack said out loud. "I wish I could see what's going on inside there now. I need equipment and reinforcements. Perhaps Norma Jean can help me out."

He watched the townhouse until it became lunch time but there was no activity that he could see. Now he believed he had solved the mystery of where Adrian went during the day and it was not to any job. Figuring he was unable to do any more there for the time being, he got ready to go to Clyde's for lunch. Before he left, he wrote down the car license number so he could find out the identity of the woman. He wanted to nail Adrian Daniels more than ever now. Surely Jessica's friend would help him. As he drove away, he drove a little faster than the speed limit. In the back of his mind was the creeping thought that Jessica was in serious danger with this man.

Chapter 20

The business was slow at Clyde's when Jack arrived for lunch. He was glad to see Norma Jean working at the counter. Quickly, he sat down at the counter and signaled to her to come over.

"Hey, Jack! I'm surprised to see you here. Did Jessica get off to North Carolina all right?"

"Sure did, Norma Jean. They left yesterday morning."

"Good, good, but say why didn't you go with them? I thought your job had been to find her and get her back to see her uncle before he died."

"That's right and we believed that was all we needed to do. Since then something else has come up. I'd like to talk to you about it. Do you get a lunch break soon?"

"In about fifteen minutes. Why?"

"I don't want to discuss it here at the counter where so many can hear. Maybe you could join me at one of the booths. It'd be more private there. That is if you are truly Jessica's friend and wouldn't mind helping her and me out."

"Now you got my curiosity up. Sure I'm her friend and no one better say any different. Ok, I'll be over there in a few minutes. What can I bring you? It'll be on the house."

"Oh, I guess I'll have today's special. While I'm waiting, a cup of coffee and a blueberry muffin would be nice."

Jack took the cup of coffee and muffin from the waitress and sat over in the booth in the corner. It was slightly withdrawn from the other tables and seemed like the best place for a private conversation. He did not want anyone else to hear his plans for investigating Adrian Daniels. One could never be too cautious in cases like this. Soon Norma Jean came over to the table with two plates of fried chicken, fries, and a biscuit. She also brought a pot of steaming coffee.

"All right, now, here is the food and I got plenty of time to listen to anything you say. Clyde said it was ok by him."

"Fine, this chicken looks great. I'm starved. Is it all right if I eat a little first before talking?"

"Sure, go ahead, I'm kind of hungry myself. I usually say a blessing before I eat so if you don't mind, I'll pray out loud for God's blessing on our food and His wisdom for our talk."

Jack nodded his head and listened while she prayed. He had missed the prayers before a meal like Jonathan always insisted on doing whenever or wherever they ate. Both of these Christians talked to God so naturally just like they knew Him personally. When this business was over, he decided he had to ask his friend to explain that to him. After the blessing, the two people ate their food in silence.

When they were both finished and a new cup of coffee had been poured, Jack said, "You asked me the reason, I stayed behind. To be honest with you, both Jonathan and I didn't quite like what we saw of Adrian Daniels. I have been checking up on him."

" Is that so? Well to be even more honest with you, I wouldn't trust that man any further than I could throw him. Jessica has told me some pretty strange things he has done since they were married."

"Like what?"

"First of all, he has been making like he has all the money in the world. Then she overhears him talking like he's on the verge of bankruptcy. And then there's a woman who keeps popping up around here. He says she's a client of his or something."

"Is she a young, nice looking red head?"

"Sure is. Have you seen her?"

"I just came from a townhouse not far from here where I've been watching Adrian and her taking a 'meeting'. It didn't look very professional to me."

"He's at a townhouse with another woman? He told Jessica that he was going to work a lot of hours while she was gone. I wonder how long this has been going on."

"Apparently for some time, I'm afraid. I went to see the investment firms in the city to find out where he worked. When I found the company that had employed him, I learned that he had been fired some months ago. He's been playing your friend for a fool. Right now all I can figure is somehow he found out about her inheritance and wants in on it. I just don't know how."

"You know I suspect that's why he was in an all fired hurry to get Jessica to make out a will. It was the day they got back from their honeymoon that he took her to a lawyer. Why the will was all ready and she signed it. We just figured he was being cautious, that's all. But still, I was a mite skeptical. Now from what you told me, maybe more so."

"Only now, I feel kind of guilty, like I know something, I should tell my best friend. I can't do that. Why it would just about kill her. He is no good but for a strange reason she loves him."

"It doesn't matter what we do, she is going to be hurt. Since he knows about her inheritance and he is involved with another woman, I'm more convinced than ever that Jessica is in danger. We have got to act fast. I need all the help I can get if I'm to nail this guy before it is too late. Will you be willing to help? It won't be easy and it might be dangerous."

"You know I will. Today has been real slow here at the deli. Clyde will give me the afternoon off if I ask him. Hey, maybe he could be of some help. He knows a lot of people in this town. Do you mind if I ask him to come over and you can tell him what is going on? He loves that young girl like a daughter though he won't admit it."

"Great, I've got a lot of leads and not enough time to get it all done by myself. Yeah, ask him to come over."

Norma Jean went into the kitchen. A few moments later, she and Clyde came out and sat down in the booth opposite Jack. He then repeated all he had learned about Jessica's husband and what had to be done. As he was talking, Clyde's face got redder and redder.

At the conclusion, Clyde said, "I knew that guy was no good. He's going to have me to deal with if he hurts Jess. Just tell us what to do and we'll help."

"Well, now, I'd better tell you that I'm not sure how far Adrian will go. We're talking big bucks here and people have killed for less. There are a lot of risks involved. What I need done may be slightly illegal. Are you still game?"

Both Clyde and Norma Jean nodded their heads and said, "You bet we are."

Jack smiled at the two friends of Jessica and knew they would help a lot. He outlined his plan for bugging the townhouse to hear just what they were planning. Clyde and Norma Jean needed to drive over there in two hours and he would instruct them further.

Driving by the motel, Jack picked up the equipment he needed before driving to the car rental company. There he exchanged the car for a panel van. He then drove to a parking space in front of townhouses under renovation and in sight of Adrian's place. Soon he was joined by his two companions.

"First of all, what I have in these suitcases is surveillance equipment, bugs if you prefer. We really need to find out just what is happening inside that townhouse. Your job is to get it inside. It won't be too hard but it will have to be when Adrian is away because he'll recognize both of you."

"Now, Norma Jean, what I want you to do is to drive your car up to the front of her house, get out and lift the hood. I will have sprayed some oil on your engine so it will appear to be smoking. Then you go to the door and ask her if you can use her phone to call for help. Tell her your car is broken down and you need to call your husband for help. If she lets you in, dial weather or the time and pretend you are talking to someone."

"While she is not looking, unscrew the mouthpiece and put this disc inside. If you can do so unobserved, take this second disc, peel off the backing, stick in under a table or something in the living room. Thank her and go out to the car. Clyde will drive up and will pretend to work on the car. The oil will have burnt off by then. Both of you drive off, park over on the next block, and rejoin me here at the van. Do you think you can do that? It'll take some fancy acting on your part."

"I'm sure I can. But I will admit I'm a little scared. I just hope she doesn't recognize me from the diner. She came in there a few times."

"I hadn't thought of that. Don't worry if she recognizes you. Just go through with it. Clyde, you can wear your hat. It will work."

They had to wait another half an hour before, Adrian's car pulled away from the townhouse. Then Norma Jean went into her act and was ushered into the townhouse. Soon Clyde met her at her car and then they both drove away. Jack only had to wait a few minutes before his fellow conspirators rejoined him in the back of the van. The plan had worked to perfection and she was sure that the other woman had not recognized her or Clyde. Both of the bugs were in place and now all they had to do was wait for Adrian to return. At four o'clock, his car stopped in front of the townhouse and he went inside.

Switching on the machine, they waited to hear what was going on inside. What they heard sent chills up their spines.

"Betty, get me a drink. I'm going to need it if you plan to make love again today. I'm really tired from earlier."

"Sure, honey."

There was a long silence before she spoke again, "Adrian, is it going to work out? How much longer do I have to share you with your wife?"

"Hey, baby, don't you worry about it. It won't be long now."

"You've said that before, too. This sneaking around is giving me the creeps."

"I don't like it anymore than you do, but we can't quit now. I know we are on the verge of being rich. Even richer than we can imagine."

"You mean she's going to be rich. Where will that leave me, your girl on the side?"

"Well, I'll tell you again because I enjoy telling of my conquests. First of all, she's down in Hickory and you're here. You've got me and my heart. When she comes back, she'll be in line for a lot of money when the old man dies. From what my sources say, he doesn't have much longer to live."

Laughing he continued, "Now here's the best part. When she gets the money, she'll have to share it with me, her loving husband - share and share alike, that's the law. Then if there should be a little accident and she unfortunately dies, it will all be mine. Maybe I should say ours."

"You're a genius! It sounds dangerous."

"Only to her, baby, only to her!"

The sound of their laughter made each one of them angry and afraid for their friend. Norma Jean looked out of the window and she began to cry softly. Jack reached over and patted her hand.

"Jack, just how much money are they talking about? How does he know so much?"

"I don't know exactly but my employer and Jessica's uncle, Mr. Garland is a very wealthy man. Years ago, he divorced his wife who got custody of their only child, a son. Since then he changed his will to include Jessica and her mom. As he is dying, he wanted to see her again and tell her of her inheritance."

"That is wonderful news for Jessica."

"What worries me though is how did Adrian find out? We did not tell him very much. There must be someone in North Carolina giving him this information. I don't know who it is but I aim to find out."

Clyde began to wave his arms. "They're talking again. Listen!"

"Adrian, do you have to go? I get so lonely here by myself."

"Yes, darling but I'll come back. I need to be home if she should call. We're so close. I can't wait to hear how things are going in Hickory. Who knows? Maybe the old man is all ready dead."

"We couldn't be that lucky."

"Our luck, as you call it, has been running pretty good, I think. Our detectives tracked her down so I could marry her. Then by sheerest good fortune, the old man sends his own detectives to find her. I was just a step ahead of them is all. But soon it will be all over and I'll have what is rightfully mine. Do you know what that is?"

"Do tell me. You seem to enjoy gloating over all this."

"You, the sweetest lover of all time, and a fortune. What could be better?"

"Please stay, Adrian! Maybe she won't call."

"Oh, she'll call all right. Remember she is madly in love with me, and I'm sure she must miss me. Maybe I want to hear her voice."

"Get out and wait for her to call! What do I care?"

"You care a whole lot, baby, especially as I am about to come into a lot of that stuff we both love, money."

At the sound of the door closing, Jack turned off the tape recorder. Now they knew how he found out about the money. No wonder there had been someone always a step ahead of them in their search. The unanswered question was still how did he find out that Mr. Garland had changed his will to include Jessica and her mother.

The three people in the van decided to take up shifts to listen to the wire taps and record every word that was said. Norma Jean said that she had to get home and fix supper for her family. She would bring Clyde and Jack some supper back. Their problem now was how would they tell Jessica the awful news. They had no choice because her life was in danger.

CHAPTER 21

Jessica thought she had only closed her eyes for a moment. The room was now shaded in the darkness of the evening twilight and she realized she had been sleeping for hours. Now, she felt rested and ready for company. Her stomach also reminded her that it was time for supper. Getting up, she changed into a dark blue skirt and white blouse. Then she stood in front of the mirror on the dresser and combed her hair. She wanted to look her best when she met her uncle.

Leaving her room, she went into the hallway. It was easy for her to find her way down into the kitchen. Only Jonathan was in the room and he turned to her with a smile and said, "Did you have a good nap, Jessica?"

"Yes, I feel much better and also very hungry. What's for supper?"

"We're having chicken and rice. I understand it's William's own recipe with a taste of the South. Here, sit down! William just took a tray up to your uncle's room. When he comes back down, he'll put supper on the table for us. We thought we'd eat here in the kitchen tonight so it'd be less trouble for William."

"That's fine with me. I like eating in the kitchen. That sure smells good. Perhaps I'll take a peek at it."

Just as she was lifting the lid on the pot on the stove and taking a sniff, William came up behind her.

"Can I get you something, Miss?"

"William! You gave me a start! I was so hungry and this chicken smells so delicious I just had to get a peek. You don't mind, do you?"

"Oh no, Miss. Just you and Jonathan have a seat at the table and I'll get the food there. We can have a cozy supper before you go up to see your uncle. He is so anxious to see you that he did not want to eat his supper first. He looked very well and rested."

They sat down at the table and watched as the butler placed a large casserole of chicken and rice, a green salad, and a plate of hot biscuits in front of them. As he sat down, he said, "Now, Jonathan, if you will say a blessing, we can eat."

They bowed their heads as Jonathan thanked the Lord for the food and their safe trip. He also said a short prayer for Mr. Garland's health. After the "amen", they all ate heartily. Jessica enjoyed the company of the two men and was glad she had come. However, she kept thinking about seeing her uncle and was a little apprehensive about the meeting.

After the meal, Jessica sat outside her uncle's bedroom door waiting to see him. She thought about the time she had spent with him as a little girl. Her memories were of the stories he told and how kind he was to her. Now her thoughts were on what she would say to him and why he wanted to see her so much. It was still somewhat of a mystery as to why he had gone to so much trouble sending Jonathan and Jack looking for her mother and her. She had an idea that he was leaving some money to her but how much was uncertain. She prayed that God would give her the right words to say.

Just then, the door opened and William motioned for her to come in the room. Taking her by the arm he whispered, "Just a short while tonight, Miss. He won't admit it but he is weak and needs rest. Maybe tomorrow you can have a longer visit. I'll be right outside the door if you need me."

At first, she thought he was asleep because he did not look up when the door closed behind her. She almost called out to William but he opened his eyes and smiled at her. Here was the kindly uncle she remembered and she returned his smile.

"Come over closer, Jessica! I can't believe you've finally come back to see me. It's been so long."

"Yes, it has been too long, Uncle."

She sat down in the chair next to his bed and noticed the old man had tears in his eyes. He grasped her hands and patted them a few times. For a while, this was all he did and she waited on him to speak.

"Jessica, I was so sad and sorry to hear about the death of your mother. She was a wonderful and special woman. Have you been all right?"

"Thank you for your concern. I suppose I've been all right. I recently married a wonderful man. I had been working and saving my money to go to college. Now, I'll be able to go there next year. Adrian, my husband, has promised me that."

The old man made a gulping sound as she mentioned her husband's name. He gasped out in a whisper, "Adrian, Adrian. What an unusual name. Did you know..."

He paused for a moment and closed his eyes. For a moment, she wondered whether she should call William into the room. She said, "Know what, Uncle?"

"Oh, nothing, my dear. We can talk about that tomorrow. Tonight I have more important matters to discuss with you."

"Reach in that second drawer of the desk over there, Jessica. There is a paper I want you to look over."

Jessica went to the desk and opened the drawer and found a black folder. Holding it up so he could see, the old man nodded his head and smiled. She brought it back to the bed and opened the folder. Inside were papers and the heading on the top sheet read, "Last Will and Testament of Thomas A. Garland".

"Yes, my dear, it's my will. Now don't look shocked. I know perfectly well what I've done here. I wanted to leave something for your mother and you. I just wished I had helped you both out a long time ago when your mother was alive. Who knows, she might still be alive now if I had. I guess I was too selfish in those days."

"Anyhow, one of the reasons I was looking for you was to show you my will. I've got quite a lot of money and soon much of it will be yours. Better that you get it than my wife and my worthless son."

"You didn't need to do this. You just can't cut them out like that. After all they are your family, much closer than me."

"It is good of you to feel that way. Don't worry, I didn't leave them out - just gave them a mite or two. You will be getting the bulk of it, though. William will have this house and enough to live well. He can sell the house and still be ahead."

"Thank you, but are you sure you want to give me all this?"

"Of course, I do. Anyhow, it is my money and I'll do what I please with it. Take the folder with you and ask Jonathan to go over it with you. He can explain all the legal terms and words to you. We can talk more about it tomorrow but for right now, I have something more important to discuss with you."

"All right. What is that?"

"As you know, I don't have a lot of time left on this earth. I've disappointed doctors at least two or three times when they said I was about to die. But this time, I'm afraid they're right. I've had a full and good life but one thing is missing. It is something your mother told me about Jesus. Can you tell me?"

"Well, what did you have in mind?"

"Your mother was always talking about how Jesus had saved her and she was going to Heaven some day. She was sure of it. Kept asking me if I knew where I'd go when I died. Well, I never gave her a straight answer or one that made sense. Mostly, I'd say that I didn't believe in that religion stuff but she never stopped talking about it. Now I wished I'd listened to her. Can you tell me how I can know about going to Heaven?"

"I'm not sure but I'll try. It has been a while since I thought much about it myself. I'll need a Bible. Mine is in my room. Perhaps William can get it for me."

"Don't bother, William. He'll say I need to go to sleep and make you leave. Pull out that drawer in the night stand right beside you. There is one there."

She opened the drawer he indicated and found a Bible. It was a paper back copy of the New Testament. At once, she recognized it as one of the copies her mother always gave to her patients. She had a large box full of them and had said she wanted to make her patients healthy spiritually as well as physically. Just holding the little book brought back memories and tears to her eyes. As she looked at it, she prayed silently, "Oh, Lord, I'm so sorry I have been neglecting you. Please forgive me. I remember what my mother taught me. Please help me tell my uncle before it is too late for him. Thank you."

The old man reached and touched her hand. "Your mother gave me that book when she left here. You recognized it, I can see that. I'm sad to say I shoved it in that drawer and that's where it stayed. At least until a few months ago when the doctor said there was little hope for me lasting much longer so I took it out and read some of it. I admit I can read long and impressive legal briefs and documents but I can't make heads or tails out of this book. Will you help me?"

"Of course, I will. Let me show you what Mother taught me years ago. I'll be reading some verses in the epistle to the Romans. God's plan for man's salvation is a gift that all of us need to accept. My first verse is Romans 3:23."

As she turned the pages of the small testament, she noticed her uncle leaning closer to see. She turned in her chair and held the book out for him to see.

"From this verse we see that men have sinned and come short of God's glory. They cannot on their own reach God. I don't have to prove to you that men are sinful, do I?"

"You don't have to tell me. I know all about the bad things people do to each other. I know how I am but what can I do?"

"Another verse, Romans 6:23 says that 'The wages of sin is death...' When we sin and turn away from God, the outcome is death. It sounds hopeless, doesn't it?"

Her uncle only nodded his head in silence, so she continued, "It's the second part of that verse which gives us hope. Do you see? It says, '...but the gift of God is eternal life through Jesus Christ, our Lord.' The next verse is Romans 5:8 which says, 'God commended His love towards us in that while we were yet sinners, Christ died for us.' This is God's love and gift to us. We don't need to get good for God to save us. He wants to give us life not death even though no one deserves it. Do you understand so far?"

"Yes, I know I don't deserve such a wonderful gift as that. Please continue!"

"In order to get a gift, it has to be accepted. In Romans 10:13, it says, 'For whosoever shall call on the name of the Lord shall be saved.' You need to receive this gift from God to be saved and go to Heaven. Jesus said in John 14:6 that He is the only way to God. There is no other."

"That's it. I wasn't sure but that's it. Tell me what I must do now. I've got so little time left."

"You need to confess or admit to God you are a sinner first of all and cannot reach Him on your own. Then you can accept Jesus Christ's death on the cross in your place as payment for your sins. Only then can you call on the Lord for salvation. Your promise is that God in His love sent Jesus to die so that you can live. John 3:16 says, 'For God so loved the world that He gave His only begotten Son, that whosoever believeth in Him should not perish but have everlasting life.' Would you like to receive Jesus tonight, Uncle Thomas?"

For a moment the old man was silent and looked away from her. When he turned to face her again, she saw tears in his eyes. In those minutes, she prayed he would accept the Lord.

Finally in a whisper, he spoke, "Your mother shared those verses with me. When you read them just now, I could remember them just like she had read them yesterday. Now they aren't so foolish as I thought back then. I needed to hear them again. God must be speaking since you gave me the very same words she did. Yes, yes, I do want Jesus. I don't know how to pray. Can you help me?"

"Yes, I'll be glad to help you. Just put what I told you in your own words. God doesn't expect some fancy prayer or big words. Just ask Him, He'll listen and answer."

He nodded his head and in his own words prayed, "Dear God, I know I have not talked to you before now. I'm such a rotten sinner that I never thought You'd want to hear from me. Right now I agree with You that I am a sinner and hopeless and about to die. Thank you for loving me and sending Jesus to die on the cross for me. I accept His death in my place as full payment for me. Please save me, Lord Jesus! I believe in You! Thank you Lord, thank You. Amen."

He looked up at her and smiled with a look of hope in his eyes. It was the most honest prayer she had ever heard. Out loud she prayed, "Thank You, Lord, thank You. Please draw us closer to yourself. Thank You for allowing me to be here and see You save my uncle. Amen."

She took his hand and said, "You are one of God's children now. He will do as He promised. This is so wonderful. Now I know why He wanted me to come here and it wasn't because of the money."

"You're right, Jessica. Thank you so much. I feel at peace now when I didn't before."

"It wasn't me but Jesus, Uncle Thomas. He turned everything to His Will just so you'd call on Him in time."

For the rest of the visit, she read some key verses of Scripture mostly from the Gospel of John. She tried her best to answer his questions but more often than not she had to admit she did not know. She promised him she would look up the answers in her Bible before her next visit.

All too soon, William came back into the room to tell her it was time to leave. She promised him she would come and see him the next morning to read some more of the Bible to him. He smiled and patted her hand before he slipped back down in his bed.

Outside the door, she paused and said a prayer of thanksgiving for her uncle's salvation. As she walked, she could hear the two men talking and her uncle sounded very happy. She was excited about the prospect of visiting him the next morning.

Chapter 22

In the hall, Jessica sat down and looked through the will that her uncle gave her. When she saw the section which described the amount of money he was leaving to her, she could not believe what she was reading. Immediately, she went downstairs to see if Jonathan was still up. She wanted to show him the will and get his advice. This was quite a shock to her. One day soon, she would be a wealthy woman.

She found Jonathan in the living room looking through a magazine. Smiling, he stood up and motioned her to sit down next to him on the sofa. At that moment, she felt that she really noticed him. This was a handsome man who was also a Christian and gentleman. The jeans and tee shirt he was wearing showed off his athletic body perfectly. For a moment, she almost forgot she was married as she sat down next to him.

"How's he doing, Jessica? Was he able to tell you very much?"

"Yes, he gave me quite a shock. But I suspect you knew it all along. He gave me a copy of his will. I just can't believe he'd leave me all that money. Why? Do you know?"

"It's not so hard to imagine. He has been trying to make things right before he dies. When he asked me to go look for you and your mother, he said he wanted to show his gratitude for your mother's kindness to him and do something kind himself."

"I can understand that. You should have known her. She had no enemies and was always helping others. Just knowing her was to love her. But I don't see why he cut his wife and son out with so little. Surely there is enough for it to be shared equally."

"Perhaps I can answer that question, Miss Jessica."

They had noticed that William had come into the room. He sat opposite them and put the tray he was carrying on the table.

He continued, "You would not say that if you knew his ex-wife and son. Years ago which was about two years after I had begun my service to Mr. Garland, they walked out on him and never looked back. It wasn't all their fault because he neglected them a lot. He worked long hours and made sure they lacked for nothing. When he was off, he went out hunting or fishing with his friends."

"Didn't his son go with him? That seems like a good way for a father and son to be together."

"It could have been but the boy was sickly when he was small. His mother would not allow him to go. As he got older, he clung to her and refused anything his father asked him to do. Mr. Garland just went right on with his life and left the boy with his mother. It was a big mistake."

"What happened then, William?"

"She eventually left him for another man. Probably a man she was able to control and do as she wished. The divorce was quick and costly to him but he seemed to be glad to be rid of them. Anyhow, your mother and father were great helpers to him during that time. They were very wonderful to him. When you were born, he came to the hospital to see you. It was a happy time for him."

"I didn't know that."

"Yes, Miss, he thought you to be such a beautiful child. Your family moved away and then we heard your father had died. We were sad at that news. It wasn't long after that he became so gravely ill with the heart problems and you and your mother came to live with us. Those were some of his happiest days for him and me in this house. So you see why he wanted to share his wealth with you now."

"It is still so sad for a family to be torn apart like that. Perhaps he might get in touch with them now so they can be reconciled. I mean he went to a lot of trouble to find me. Maybe he could get in touch with them before he dies."

William only shook his head and said, "We have tried but his wife only told her lawyer that she was only interested in the reading of the will. No, they will not be reconciled. That part of his life is gone. Well, I better take this tray back to the kitchen and get all that cleaned up before I retire for the night. Call me if either of you need anything. Good night."

They watched him as he left the room. Jonathan finally spoke, "Well now, you were in the old man's room for a long time. Did he have anything else to say?"

"Oh, yes, I should have told you this first because it is so much more important than money and wills and such. I was able to lead my uncle to the Lord. He was saved."

"Wow - that's great news. I've been praying for him ever since I first met him."

"Well, if the Lord allows him a little time now, maybe he might just forgive and get back together with his wife and child."

"We could pray for that if you like. In fact, why don't we have some prayer now!"

She readily agreed and they both bowed their heads. As he began to pray, she was a little startled that he reached over and took her hand in his. She wanted at first to pull it back but thought that might be rude. Anyhow his hands felt so warm and strong that she allowed him to hold hers. They prayed for a brief time and when he said "Amen", he did not drop her hand right away. For a moment that seemed to go on for a long time he held it. The ringing of the telephone startled them both and he let go. She was surprised at how disappointed she felt when he dropped her hand.

She jumped up quickly and ran to get the phone. Surely he had notice how red her face had become. Adrian was on the other end of the line. It was hard for her to be excited about the call as she felt guilty about just now holding another man's hand even if it was innocent and that she liked it. All too soon, she hung up the receiver and returned to the living room. She purposely sat down in a chair opposite of Jonathan.

"That was fast. Didn't Adrian have much to say?"

"No, he could only talk for a few minutes. There was an important client that he needed to see tonight. Something about a cocktail party at the man's house. He was all ready late so he promised me a longer call tomorrow night. I didn't get to tell him about my visit with my uncle, but he did inquire about his health."

Jonathan saw a strange look on the young woman's face that he was not sure was the cause. He had to admit he was sorry she had sat in the chair and not back on the sofa with him. He said, "Do you want to go over the will tonight? I would be glad to explain any questions you have."

"No, I am tired. I think I better go up to my room now. A lot has happened to me and I need some time to think. Uncle Thomas asked a lot of questions that I couldn't answer and I need to try and find the answers before I talk to him again tomorrow."

"All right. It is getting late. I'll see you in the morning."

She rose quickly and almost ran up the stairs. He watched her as she left. It was difficult for him to ignore his feelings about her and remember she was a married woman. Her hand had felt so good while he had held it. If only she had not rushed into the marriage. If only she was still available.

"Nonsense," he finally said out loud in a whisper. She was married and that was not going to change now. All he wanted to do was to be her friend and help her out as much as he could. The secret that was being revealed by Jack's investigation was not making it any easier for him. For her sake, he still hoped everything would work out for the best for her.

Upstairs, Jessica hastily dressed for bed and sat down with her Bible in the comfortable rocking chair. She could not forget the kind and tender touch of the man downstairs. To get those thoughts out of her mind, she began to read her Bible at the book of John. However, she did not get very far in her reading. Soon she had so many memories of her mother and her in that very room that she gave up on her reading and let herself remember.

She saw her mother sitting and rocking while reading a Bible story or praying with her at bedtime. Suddenly she felt tired and decided to go to bed. Even there she lay awake thinking of her mother until she finally fell asleep. Her dreams were not of her mother or of her uncle but Jonathan kept entering into them at the oddest places. Her night's rest was not peaceful.

For the next two days, she spent most of her time with Jonathan. He had explained all the provisions of the will in a clear, concise way. While her uncle rested, they took long walks and talked about his plans for the future as a lawyer. He hoped to one day open his own office, but that dream would be a long time coming. She told him about how she wanted to go back to school and train to be a nurse. Many times though they discussed what she had read in her Bible or a question which her uncle had asked her. It was good to talk the questions out with Jonathan who helped her to formulate a better answer. She was beginning to like the time spent with this young man even more than she felt she should.

The rest of her time was spent with her uncle. They reminisced about the time she stayed with him. He even told her some stories she had not heard about her father and mother. In between the stories, she read to him from her Bible and did her best to answer his questions. No mention was ever made of his family or of her life back in Harrisonburg.

She was enjoying her visit and did not feel in a hurry to go home. When Adrian called her each evening, she made an excuse as to why she had to spend one more day. He encouraged her to spend as much time as she wanted with her uncle and not to worry about him. He was being well taken care of at home.

While she was visiting her uncle, Jonathan was busy talking to Jack about the investigation. He had been successful at bugging the townhouse and had been sending copies of the tapes each day. Since he did not want to have Jessica overhear the tapes, he went to Jack's office to listen to them. Each day he became more and more concerned about Jessica's safety. He was glad that she decided to stay there while he could sort out just what was going on.

He reported to William who sorted out how much he told his employer each day. They felt he was too weak to bear the full news of Jack's findings. Both of them were sick to hear what was on the tapes and did not know how to tell Jessica. Both of them decided that she would not go back to Adrian until they knew the whole story.

On the third day, the package he received from Jack was particularly disturbing. He waited until Jessica was visiting her uncle before he showed it to William. Over their morning cup of tea and coffee, they listened to the tape from the townhouse.

"Adrian, how long is it going to take? I'm not going to wait around for you forever?"

"Hey, we've been all through that. It's almost over. She's gone down to see the old man. According to my lawyer, Mason, he's all but gone now."

"I know that. How will you get the money? What if she finds out who you are?"

"It won't help her one bit. She and I are married."

"She could divorce you."

"Are you kidding? She's a Christian remember! She'd die before she'd do that."

"Hey, that's not a bad idea!"

"Seriously, honey, she's bound to find out. Won't you go to the funeral? After all, he is your father."

"My father, what a joke! He never cared about me or my mother. His career was always first. When he wasn't working he'd be out in the woods somewhere proving his manhood or something by shooting animals. He tried to take me with him but I hated it. What a waste of time! Then he threw us out with enough money to barely live on. Why I don't know what we'd done if it hadn't been for Ed. He's more of a father to me. Now my father is only giving us a few crumbs in his will."

"How can you be sure? Maybe he has had a change of heart?"

"Him! Never! He hates us, and I hate him. I hope he dies slowly and painfully. Anyhow, Mason has been keeping us informed about any changes in my father's will. He's a partner at the law firm as well as my mother's lawyer. It was a stroke of genius to get him into the firm so he was able to look out for our interests all these years. There have been no changes."

"Well, then let's celebrate and have a drink for all the lovely money you'll get. Where does that leave me? You're married. I can't stand the thought of you and her together every night."

"Hey, I don't love her. You know you're my woman. Whenever I kiss her or make love to her, I close my eyes and pretend it's you. Hey, come over here and let me show you what love is."

"Stop it, Adrian. I can't go on like this. You've got to choose, either her or me."

"Look, it's all under control. My mother has a fool proof plan. He thought I wouldn't get all his money, but I will. When she gets back, we're going to arrange a little accident. We'll wait a respectable period and then you'll be a very rich Mrs. Adrian Daniels."

"You mother's the smart one all right. Imagine her pretending to be your housekeeper. That was a stroke of genius."

"You better believe it. I can't wait to break the news to my wife. Won't it be a scream! Of course, it will be the last laugh - the very last laugh for her."

"Honey, I'm scared."

"Don't be. It will be over soon. Look, I've got to get back to the house. I'll let you know when anything happens. Good night."

"Good night, Adrian. I'll be dreaming about you."

They heard the sound of a door closing after a few moments and decided to turn off the tape machine. Both of them sat in stunned silence as the words they had heard began to make sense to them. They were glad Jessica had not heard it.

After a moment William spoke, "I can't believe it. Jessica's husband is Mr. Garland's son. How did it happen? It is too fantastic. How, Jonathan?"

"It answers a lot of questions I have had all along. Mr. Mason at the firm has been keeping them up to date. He must have sent out detectives to find Jessica and her mother also. No wonder there was always someone just ahead of us at each turn. He would have access to all the papers there as well as Mr. Garland's will."

"The last piece of the puzzle is in place and it only shows danger for Jessica. Adrian is his son. It had only been a masquerade to get his hands on his father's money."

"What do we do now, Jonathan?"

"After Jessica comes out of her uncle's room, I must tell him about what we have found out. You need to call Jack and tell him to go to the police and tell them what he suspects. Also he needs to get as much evidence as he can and wait until I let him know our next move."

"What about Jessica? How much can we tell her?"

"We will tell her nothing just now. Under no circumstances will she go back home alone. I don't care what it takes but Adrian won't hurt her. Not if I have anything to say about it."

Chapter 23

Early the next morning, Jonathan left the house to run some errands for Mr. Garland. Last night, he had a long briefing with his employer about the tape which Jack had sent to them. He was surprised the old man had taken the news so well about his son and ex-wife. They both agreed to wait on telling Jessica until there was more proof, and she was to be protected at all costs. Mr. Emery, his law partner, was to be informed about Mason's activities. He was to make copies of the tapes as soon as possible.

The only other person who was awake when he left was William who offered him some breakfast. He refused, saying he would get something downtown. Before leaving, he made the butler promise not to say anything to Jessica about her husband.

William watched him drive away while he fixed the old man's breakfast tray and morning medicine. It seemed odd to him that his employer had not rung for him. Usually, he was the first one to wake up and always called. The butler figured the news of the previous night had caused him to oversleep. He decided to take the tray to him anyway and see if he was all right.

It was dark and silent in the room as he entered. His employer did not move when he came into the room. After he had turned on the light and took a closer look at the man in the bed, it was apparent he had died during the night. A peaceful look with a slight smile was what William would always remember about finding the old man. He pulled the covers over his face and stood there for a moment. It was too late to call any help so he wanted to pay his final respects in private. He wept for the man who been his employer and friend. All too soon, he made the necessary telephone calls.

When Jonathan returned to the house, the ambulance was just pulling away. He ran inside to find William and Jessica talking to another man who he recognized as Mr. Garland's doctor. When Jessica saw him, she ran over and threw her arms around him. Pulling her close to him, he held her while she wept on his shoulder. Being so close to her felt good and he wanted to keep on holding her.

Jessica backed away as if she suddenly realized who was next to her. For an instant she looked right into his eyes. No words were spoken but she felt a longing to touch him again. When he reached out to her, she shook her head and walked away. This was confusion to her for she was a married woman. How could she long for another man's touch? Her husband had not held her so tenderly for a long time. Hastily, she went into the living room.

Jonathan stood there watching her, seeing a question on her face before she turned away. Did she sense his feelings for her when he held her? He had tried so hard to hide it from her. He knew those feelings were wrong and a horrible sin against God. Now he was confused because for a moment he felt she was returning those feelings. This was all wrong but what could he do? Right then he knew he must protect her from all harm, especially her husband.

William broke the silence by saying, "Excuse me, Jonathan. I didn't mean to ignore you but I needed to make arrangements about Mr. Garland."

"That's all right, William. What has happened? I saw the ambulance and the doctor. Has Mr. Garland taken a turn for the worse?"

"I'm afraid he died some time last night. He never called out or anything. It seems he just passed away in his sleep. I found him earlier just after you left when I took him his breakfast tray. As soon as I saw his face, I knew he was gone. One thing did seem rather odd, though."

"What was that?"

"His face was so peaceful looking with a hint of a smile. It reminded me how a person looks when he sees an old friend that he has not seen for a long time. Do you know what I mean?"

Jonathan only nodded his head in agreement and looked in the living room to see if Jessica was still there. She was gone. He promised himself he would talk to her later. She needed time to sort all this out alone.

William did not notice his hesitation and went on, "Anyhow I had thought he would have been in a bad mood last night after you gave him that awful news about you know what. He wasn't however. Actually he seemed happy in a way. He kept telling me about how he had asked Jesus to save him a couple nights ago and soon he would be in Heaven with Him. I did not think a whole lot about it last night. Today, with him dead and looking so peaceful, I cannot get it out of my mind. Is he in Heaven right now?"

"Yes, I believe that is exactly where he is at this very minute. You can also have that kind of assurance, too, you know."

"Well, Jonathan, it is confusing. I was always taught you lived by the Bible's rules and morals. If you did the best you could, God would take you into His Heaven when you died. There was no way you could know until then."

"Let's sit here in the living room, William and I'll try and explain what I meant. I've got a New Testament so we can look up the verses. Your question is even here in the Bible. The Philippian jailer asked Paul in the sixteenth chapter of Acts. Here it is in verse thirty. 'Sirs, what must I do to be saved?' Isn't that your question also?"

"Yes, it is. I do believe I would like to know the same thing for myself."

"You can read the answer for yourself because it is in the next verse."

"All right, verse thirty-one says, 'And they said, Believe on the Lord Jesus Christ and thou shalt be saved and thy house.'"

For a moment neither man spoke or moved. William read the verse again silently before saying, "But, that is so simple. Is that all there is to it? I have believed about Jesus all my life. It has never given me any assurance other than some good feelings when I go to church. I want what Mr. Garland believed which caused him to die so peacefully."

"You're right it is simple, but your belief has to be more than just acknowledging you believe Jesus was a real person and the Bible is about Him. In fact, the Bible says the demons believe that much. No, it's a commitment of your life to Him and accepting His death on your behalf to pay the penalties for your sins.."

For the next half hour, Jonathan shared verses from Romans with the older man. William interrupted many times with questions which he was able to answer from the Bible. Finally, William held up his hand and said, "Wait a minute, Jonathan. You mean if I acknowledge I am a sinner and ask Jesus to be my Savior, He will save me?"

"Yes, He will. God wants all men to be saved. It says so right here in II Peter 3:9 that He wants no one to perish.

Today is the day on which God is calling you to receive eternal life. Will you accept God's gift now? We can pray right here."

"Yes, I would. I want to see Mr. Garland again but most of all I want to know Jesus who loves me so much."

Both men bowed their heads and knelt down by the sofa. In those few minutes, another soul was added to the kingdom of God.

"Thank you, Jonathan. Now I know why he looked so peaceful. Jesus is my Savior, too."

"Don't thank me, William. It's the Lord who should get all the credit. I was just His messenger in this."

"You are right. I have got to get busy and make all the arrangements for the funeral. I could use some help if you do not mind."

"Not at all. Let's brew some coffee and get right to it."

The rest of the morning, William and Jonathan made telephone calls for the funeral arrangements. They discovered the old man had specified all the details for his funeral and burial with the funeral home. All had been paid in full. It would be done the next afternoon.

Jonathan made the call to his law office. According to instructions left by Mr. Garland, his will was to be read right after the burial. Both partners agreed to come right away to pay their respects. After hanging up the telephone, Jonathan said, "Wow, that was quick work. But why did he want to be buried so soon?"

"That was the way he wanted it. He did not think many people would come anyway so he did not want it to be dragged out. He always wanted to get things arranged quickly and completely."

"He sure did. I just wish I could have gotten to know him better. I'm sure we would have been friends."

"He was a good man, really. We will see him again in Heaven."

"You're right. I suppose though we'll have to notify his family. We both know where they are."

"No, let's just let the two partners in the firm take care of that. Mr. Mason will probably represent them. I do not believe they will come here."

"That would blow their whole scheme if Jessica found out who they really are now. Which reminds me. I better call Jack and tell him the news. He will want to come to the funeral tomorrow."

"When will we tell Jessica?"

"I don't know even know how I'm going to tell her, much less when. The best time will be after the funeral and the reading of the will. Do you agree?"

"It will be a terrible shock to her."

"Yes, William, it will be devastating to say the least. I received another package of tapes from Jack and I fear the worst for her. I'd rather have Jack here when we tell her. We can then go back to Harrisonburg with her and help confront her husband with the facts."

"I just hope she will be able to take the truth."

"Don't worry, William. She will. I believe she's a lot like her mother. Down deep, she'll find out she can be just as strong. You'll see. Anyhow I plan to stay right by her side until it is all over. No one is going to hurt her while I'm around."

"Yes, sir. We must all help her."

Chapter 24

Jessica ran to her room and threw herself on the bed. Her tears flowed freely as she thought of her dead uncle. It seemed so unfair that just as she found him again, he was gone. Her only happy thought was that he was in Heaven and she would see him again.

She remembered how Jonathan was glad to hear of her uncles' conversion. He had, in only a few days, become a good friend. He seemed so kind, warm and loving - a man any woman would want for a husband. Adrian was not like him at all, for he was hot one minute and cold the next. He loved her physically but did not seem to love her tenderly and kindly. If only, she had met Jonathan earlier.

No, how could she have those thoughts? She was married and wishing did not change those facts. Had not she always been taught marriage was a sacred vow which lasted until death? She promised herself she would be faithful to her husband no matter what or who came into her life.

Then again, how could she forget his touch when he held her in his arms only moments ago? It was an innocent gesture to comfort her in her grief. Surely it was all he felt. Why was she so confused? Why had she longed to linger in his arms and feel so safe?

The chimes from the clock in the hall put an end to her thoughts. "Oh my, I didn't realize I'd been here so long. I'm sure I can be of some help to Jonathan and William."

Down in the foyer, she found William giving orders to a large group of people. Every one was cleaning or setting up folding chairs in the parlor. Chairs and tables were removed to the back rooms. Although many people were going in and out of the room, all was organized and orderly. At that moment, the butler noticed her on the stairs. Handing a clipboard to another man and giving instructions, he came over to the stairs.

"Why, Jessica. Did you have a good rest? I hope all this noise did not disturb you."

"No, I really didn't hear anything until I came down here. Who are all these people anyway? What are they doing?"

"Mr. Garland left very specific instructions about his funeral arrangements. Since he was never a church-goer, he wanted to have a short and simple ceremony here at the house. The will reading is set for after we return from the graveside.

"As for all these people, they were hired by Mr. Garland's law firm to have everything set up. They are almost finished and then all of them will be going. Then we can have a quiet lunch before we go to the funeral home for the viewing this afternoon. I do not believe too many people will come. He kept pretty much to himself. Those lawyers will be there."

"Surely his family will come. Haven't they been notified?"

"Oh, you can be sure, Mr. Mason has been in touch with his wife and son. He is a partner in the firm as well as her personal lawyer. No, you will not see them here. When she left, she swore never to set foot in this house again. Knowing her, she will keep her word. I almost believe Mr. Garland decided to have the funeral here just so she would not attend. As far as other relations, I doubt they will come unless they hope to be named in the will."

"That is so sad. What about their share of the estate? They'll need to be here for the reading?"

"No, they will not have to be here even for the reading of the will. Their attorney will take care of all that. Oh, before I forget - Jonathan went out for a while. He had to meet with the funeral home directors to change some of the service. Since Mr. Garland accepted Jesus Christ as his Savior, he wanted to have Scripture read at the service."

Jessica ran down the stairs and stood next to William. "Did Jonathan tell you about my uncle's decision?"

"Yes, he did. He explained salvation to me this morning. I also asked Christ to be my Savior today."

"That's wonderful news, William! I'm so happy for you."

"Happy is the word for it. Now Mr. Garland's death is not nearly so sad. It is more like a short parting but I will see him again in Heaven. Right now, I want to tell everyone about Jesus. Mr. Jonathan hopes we can get a preacher to give a message with an invitation tomorrow. It will not be easy finding someone at this short notice. If he cannot, Jonathan will speak. Maybe other people will come to know Him as their Savior."

"It would be great. Oh, that man over there is trying to get your attention."

"He is the foreman for this crew. They are probably finished. If you will excuse me, I will talk to him and then we can have some lunch. We can talk some more about the Bible. Of course, if it is all right with you?"

"Sure, we can do that. I'll go to get my Bible from my room and meet you in the kitchen."

She watched as William went into the living room and sat down next to a man wearing blue coveralls. Both of them were looking at clip boards and checking off items on each one. Feeling somewhat in the way of their proceedings, she went back up to her room. There she picked up her Bible and made her way to the kitchen. She needed to look up Bible verses to share with William.

At the funeral home, Jonathan had finished talking with the funeral director. A minister friend had agreed to give a short message at the funeral and offer a prayer at the graveside.

From there, he drove to the airport to meet Jack. As he pulled into the parking lot, Jack waved and ran up to the car. Opening the door, he threw his bag into the back seat and got into the front.

"Thanks for picking me up, Jonathan. It's not a great day, is it? I'll sure miss the old man. He was like a father to me."

"We will all miss him. Even though I only knew him for a short period of time, I got to like him a lot."

"Yeah, he was like that. You either liked him or hated his guts. There was no middle ground with him. I guess I'd better stop by the funeral home and pay my respects. Then we better go somewhere to talk. I've got a lot to tell you before we break the news to Jessica."

Both men were silent as they drove the few blocks to the funeral home. They tried to reconcile their memories with their sorrow. Jack went in alone and stayed only for fifteen minutes. When he returned to the car, Jonathan noticed his eyes were a little red.

As they pulled away from the curb, Jonathan said, "Are you all right, Jack?"

"Yeah, sure, he was just special to me, that's all. It was just hard to see him there like that. I can't do anything for him now but I sure can help Jessica. It was his last wish."

Driving to Jack's office, Jonathan parked the car and followed his partner into his office. Once inside, Jack set up the tape player and sat down at his desk. From a small refrigerator behind his desk, he took out two soda cans and offered one to Jonathan. Out of his bag, he pulled two more tapes and inserted one into the machine.

"We are going to be here for a while. Why don't you call and order us a pizza, Jon. The number is right on the phone."

Jonathan took care of the lunch call and said, "Is it worse than you've told us?"

"Jonathan, I've got the goods on this guy. Let's review what we know. He is after all, Mr. Garland's son. He knows all about the will and who is getting what. Now listen to this tape. Then we will decide just what to do next."

For the next hour, they listened to tapes and ate pizza. The more they heard, the more they knew just how dangerous Adrian and his parents would be. Somehow they were planning to get rid of Jessica and take all of the estate. When they had listened to the last tape, they decided to return to the house to see Jessica. However, they both agreed to wait until after the will was read to tell her about her husband. They would make sure she was fully protected from those people.

CHAPTER 25

For Jessica, the next day went by like a dream, reality and shadows blending. She went through all the accepted movements; shaking this one's hand, receiving a hug from another and managing a weak smile at times. No one could know the confusion she felt.

The service was brief but the minister had given a clear presentation of the Gospel. Only a few people had attended the ceremonies. She was saddened that so few had cared to come and pay their last respects to her uncle. She had also hoped that his ex-wife and son would come so she could meet them.

Upon returning from the grave site, she went to her room to change before the reading of the will. It was quiet there and she had a few moments to think. It was hard for her to believe that all this was happening to her. In a few days, her life had completely changed and now she had a great fortune. Before these days, she was convinced she was in love with one man, her husband, but now she was confused. Her thoughts were more for Jonathan not Adrian. What would her life be like now? All too soon, William called her to come downstairs.

In the parlor, the workmen were already removing the chairs as she passed by on her way into the library. Inside, she was again impressed by the number of books on the shelves lining the walls. There were books on many different subjects and she wished she had the time to read them except all the books on the law.

Seated behind the desk was her uncle's partner, Mr. Emery, and next to him was the other partner, Mr. Mason. Both of them were dressed in black suits and looked every bit like lawyers. Jonathan, Jack, and William were sitting in chairs set up in front of the desk. They motioned her to sit down next to them.

It only took a short time to read the will. There were no surprises for her. The amount of money being left to her was still an amazement. While all the amounts were being read, she noticed Mr. Mason taking a lot of notes. He did not look pleased at all. Jonathan reached over and patted her hand a couple of times and smiled at her. She was so glad he was there.

Later that afternoon, Jessica decided to look around the house while waiting for William to prepare tea for them. Jack and Jonathan had gone out, leaving her to herself. She had not paid much attention to the pictures and other things in the house. Most of her time had been spent with her uncle or Jonathan.

Opening the door to her uncle's office, she decided to start where he must have spent many hours. She wanted to learn more about the man who had given her so much. At first, all the trophies overwhelmed her and she almost closed the door to look in another room. Pictures on the wall behind the desk caught her attention. Most were pictures of her uncle and other men at hunting camps. One picture made her look more than once. She could not believe her eyes. Trembling, she removed the picture from the wall to get a better look.

Still holding the picture, she called out, "William! William, please come at once! I need you!"

She sat down on the couch and kept staring at the picture. Just then, William ran into the room. He was still wearing his apron and was drying his hands on a dish towel.

"Are you all right, Jessica? I hurried because you sounded so frightened. What is wrong?"

"I'm fine, I think, William. I didn't mean to frighten you so. It's this picture. Who are these people?"

She handed it to William. He looked at the picture and said, "Why this a picture of Mr. Garland as a young man with his prize pack of beagles. Those dogs were amazing hunting animals. He was so proud of them. As I recall, it was taken right after we moved into this house in the back yard. What else did you want to know?"

"It's just he looks like..like..so much like my husband that they could twins. I don't understand?"

"Now, Miss, it could just be a coincidence, you know. There are a lot of people that look alike. I wouldn't let it worry me."

"No, it seems too close a resemblance. I don't see any pictures of my uncle's family here. I did hope they would come to the funeral. It seems so cold hearted for them not to come."

The butler sat down next to her and said, "I was not surprised not seeing them here. They never fit in or even tried to fit into your uncle's lifestyle. Oh, please, do not get me wrong, it was not just their fault. He did work long hours and took many hunting trips. His boy just never was much interested in guns or hunting. So, right or wrong, he just left the boy to his wife's care and went on with his life. Now young Adrian was a lad who liked..."

"Wait a minute, William! What did you call his son?"

"Oh, dear, I have said too much. I need to get the tea ready. Those two young men will be hungry when they return and it is too early for supper. If you will excuse me?"

"No, William. What do you mean you've said too much? You called him, Adrian. That is my husband's name. Please explain this to me."

"Maybe it would be better if we waited for Jonathan and Jack to come back to talk about this."

He stood up and started to leave. Jessica grabbed his hand and said, "Please tell me now. I have a right to know what this is all about. There is a resemblance."

"Well, Mr. Garland's son was named after him. The boy's name was also Thomas Adrian Garland just like his father. Everyone called him Adrian which was what his mother wanted. When the divorce was final and his mother remarried, he took his stepfather's name. I cannot seem to remember what that was at this time, however."

"Are there any pictures of them here? I really want to see them. It is a great coincidence if my husband looks like my uncle and also has the same name as my uncle's son."

"I still think we should wait on all this. Why not have a cup of tea and wait for Jonathan?"

"Please get those pictures for me, William. I have to see them now. I can't wait."

"Yes, Jessica. There is a photo album in the drawer in that table right next to you. Those are the only ones left in the house. They are quite a few years old."

She pulled the album out of the drawer and asked the butler to point out the pictures of her uncle's family. To her shock, there was a younger Mrs. Simms staring at her with the same scowl she always seemed to wear. The young boy standing next to her could not be anyone but her husband as a child.

"I don't understand, William. How can this be? That has to be my husband and that is our housekeeper. What is going on here? Are you keeping something from me?"

"I'm sorry you found out this way. We were going to tell you everything right after the reading of the will. They will be back any minute now, and we will tell you all we know. Come with me into the kitchen and I will fix you a hot cup of tea. It will make you feel better."

"All right, William. I certainly could use some tea after the shock I've just had. Just tell me, what was the name of the stepfather?"

"His name is Edward Daniels. The same name as your husband."

"Just one more question, please, before we go to get some tea. Does the name Simms mean anything to you?"

"Mr. Garland's wife, Nora's maiden name was Simms."

Jessica nodded her head and buried her face in her hands. There was no way she could stop the tears. William helped her up and gently guided her into the kitchen. While she sat at the table, he poured her a hot cup of tea and put it in front of her.

Just then, Jack and Jonathan came into the kitchen. She looked up at them and said, "You're back. Now will you all please tell me the truth! I have a right to know what is going on here."

Both of the two men looked at each other and sat down at the table opposite to Jessica. Jonathan was the first to speak, "All right, Jessica, what is it you want to know?"

"How long have you known that Adrian, my husband and my uncle's son was the same person? How much else do you know that you have not told me? Why didn't you tell me? I think that pretty much covers it."

"All right, we will tell you what we know. I promise you that we only had your interests at heart, though."

"Lying to me had my interests at heart. How do you figure that?"

"Okay, you have every right to be angry. We wanted to be sure of what we had before we told you. In fact, we had planned to tell you right after we returned now. Isn't that correct, William?"

William poured three more cups of tea and sat down at the table as he said, "Yes, Jessica. This was our plan. We did not want to tell you until we had all the facts. It was just an accident you saw those pictures."

Jack added, "I've been up in Harrisonburg gathering evidence on your husband while you were here. Your friends, Norma Jean and Clyde helped me. You can ask them if what we tell you is true. They are still working on it with the local police right now."

"Please believe me, Jessica, we didn't want to hurt you but only to be sure." Jonathan took her hand as he spoke.

Jessica pulled her hand back and said, "All right, I believe you were going to tell me. It still doesn't make sense to me. Why did he do this to me?"

"Greed, that is all I can say right now. Perhaps we better start from the beginning. I will begin and Jack can take up where he worked the last few days."

Taking a long sip of his tea, Jonathan began, "We were hired by your uncle to find you and your mother. At each lead we followed, we always found out that someone had been there before us asking the same questions. We followed you to Richmond where we found out about your mother's death and your move to Harrisonburg. It was then we located you through Clyde's Deli and met you at your house."

"I have to admit I was a little suspicious of your husband when we first met. I don't know why but I had to check it out. That is why Jack stayed in town while you and I came back here."

Clearing his throat, Jack said, "At first, I thought he was being a little too cautious. However, your uncle agreed I should check it out since there was a lot of money involved, and he really cared about you."

"Anyhow, I went to just about all the financial brokers in the city trying to find the one where your husband worked. I finally found out that he had been fired a few months ago for misusing funds and inappropriate conduct towards women clients and employees of the company. He has not worked at any firms since you have been married."

"He lied to me. Just where had he been going when he told me he was going to work or to see a client."

"I'm afraid here is where it gets really dirty. He has been going to a townhouse which belongs to a Miss Betty Smith. I doubt it is her real name. Anyhow that is where he spends his time. With the help of your two friends at the deli, we were able to bug the place. I have tapes of the conversations which clearly shows he knew all along who you were and that his father was going to leave you most of the estate. Would you like me to play the tapes?"

Jessica looked down at the table and asked, "What does this woman look like?"

"She's young, tall with red hair..."

"Is my husband having an affair with her? Just tell me out right."

"Yes, he is. Do you want to hear the tapes?"

"No, not now. What else did you learn? Does he want a divorce?"

"He knows you won't give him a divorce. The other thing we found out is that the housekeeper and her husband are really your husband's mother and stepfather. She is the real brains in this outfit of scoundrels."

"This still makes no sense to me. How did he find out about the will?"

Jonathan answered her, "Mr. Mason, the partner in your uncle's firm is also their lawyer and he told them. I need to inform Mr. Emery of this as soon as possible to see if there is any way we can prosecute him for that."

"That is all well and good. What am I going to do? I'm still married to him and he's not going to divorce me and lose all the money he's worked so hard to get. Didn't he think, I would find out?"

"I'm sure he did but he didn't care. They would come up with some way to do away with you so they would have it all. They're very dangerous people who will stop at nothing to get their hands on your uncle's estate."

Jonathan added, "Yes, Jessica they are dangerous. Why don't you stay here until we get it all sorted out? All three of us are willing to help you in any way we can."

Both Jack and William nodded their heads in agreement at that. Jessica was silent as she looked at all three men at the table. She felt that they had told her the truth and she could trust them. This was horrible, so unbelievable that she had been so foolish and so fooled by a man she had trusted and loved. Norma Jean was right about him and she had refused to listen to reason. Now she was going to pay for it. It was too much, she had to be alone to think.

Rising from the table, she said, "I'd like to think about this alone. I'm going to my room. Maybe later, you can play those tapes for me. Thank you for being honest with me. I know I can trust all of you."

William spoke for the three men, "That is a good idea. You get some rest and I'll call you when supper is ready."

After she left, Jack said, "We've got to stay with her from here on out. She goes nowhere without one of us going along. Agreed?"

"Agreed!" The other two said in unison. However, they were not sure just what could possibly happen next.

Chapter 26

Jessica retreated to the quiet of her room. Once inside, she fell face down on the bed and gave herself over to tears. After she had cried all she could, she sat up and began to think over all they had told her. She wondered if there was still any information they had kept back from her. When she listened to those tapes, if she found the courage to listen, she would know.

How could Adrian be so cold and cruel when she had offered him her life and love? So many things began to make sense to her. Mr. and Mrs. Simms never seemed to be servants at all and the housekeeper always had something on Adrian. Her husband getting angry whenever she questioned him about his work or where he was going.

His change of mood from being romantic to being so cold was always so frustrating to her. Now it was all too clear to her as to why he was so cold to her. He had someone else whom he cared about more than her.

Sometimes the trouble with learning the truth is not knowing how to deal with it. The evidence was too overwhelming not to be believed. She realized she had only known these men for a few days but they had no reason to lie to her. Anyhow, William was a friend from her childhood so he was trustworthy. Her only conclusion was they were telling her the truth.

Now the only question left in her mind was what was she going to do. Her marriage for all practical purposes was finished. Divorce on her part was out of the question but Adrian might not care. Somehow, she had to know for sure where she stood. Opening her door quietly, she tiptoed down the hall to the back stairs. The door to the kitchen was open and she could hear all three of the men talking. They were all still in the kitchen. This suited her plan very well.

Hurrying back to her room, she called the airline and switched her return ticket to a flight leaving in an hour. She then packed an overnight bag. She wrote a note to William and placed it on the night stand. Silently she crept down the front stairs and out the door. She planned to call a taxi from the convenience store at the end of the block. She was determined to take control of her life and confront Adrian to get the truth out of him. It did not matter anymore how much it was going to hurt. She hoped they would understand her actions.

In the kitchen, the three men were discussing their next move unaware that Jessica had left. Jack was anxious to take a direct approach to their problem of Adrian. "Why can't Jessica file a complaint against him. Throw him in jail. He deserves it."

"We can't do that, Jack. Why, the man has done nothing illegal in marrying her. Just because he has been unfaithful, no court has anything they can do against him. We don't have proof of a crime. Jessica's only recourse is a divorce."

"Jonathan is right, unfortunately." William said as her poured them all another cup of tea. "I want to get him for what he has done to Jessica. I know Mr. Garland never wanted them to have a lot of his money. Since it was his wish, I believe we must honor it. Besides they are such villains, they deserve to be thrown in the nearest jail."

"I talked to Mr. Emery this morning after the funeral. He was very shocked to learn Adrian had found out the provisions of Mr. Garland's will before it was read. According to him, only he, Mr. Garland, and one secretary knew anything about the will. He was really upset and said he'd get to the bottom of it. He's coming here this afternoon."

"That should help, Jonathan. Mr. Emery is a good ally. We need to decide a course of action soon. Do not forget Jessica's life is in danger. Neither of you really stressed that fact to her especially Adrian saying he would arrange an accident. She does not know the extent of her danger."

"Right, William, we can't lose track of that fact. I just didn't want to frighten her. We'll tell her more when she listens to the tapes tonight. We'll just let her rest for now."

The doorbell ringing interrupted their conversation. As William went to answer it, the two men drank their tea in silence. Soon, William showed two men into the kitchen, Mr. Emery and a very worried looking Mr. Mason.

Mr. Emery was the first to speak, "I'm glad to find all three of you here. Mr. Mason and I have had a long talk after the funeral. He has a lot to tell you. Should we have Jessica in on this conversation?"

"She's resting, sir and I don't plan on disturbing her for a while." William spoke up from the doorway. "Why did you bring him here, Mr. Emery? He represents that woman and her son who are causing all kinds of trouble for this household and Miss Jessica."

"I agree he doesn't deserve to be here. I know how you feel. We won't stay long. However, Jonathan, I listened to the tapes and read the notes you gave me this morning. It disturbs me greatly that confidential information leaked out of my office so easily."

"One question kept coming back to me over and over. How did they find out about the terms of Thomas' will? I did not tell anyone. Thomas certainly did not tell anyone since it was his wish to keep it secret. I can guarantee my secretary who has been with me for thirty some years can be trusted implicitly. It left only one possibility, Mason. The tapes confirmed it. I confronted him and told him, he has to tell you himself."

All eyes turned to the man standing beside Mr. Emery. At first, he looked at each face hoping to see even a glimmer of acceptance. Seeing none, he swallowed and spoke, "Yes, Phillip is correct on that score. I told them about the changes made to the will. At the time, it seemed only proper that his wife and son get a better deal. It was his wife who helped me get into the law firm in the first place. When it came time for the divorce, I represented her in court. But I never knew they'd ask anything else of me."

A while back, she heard about Mr. Garland being in poor health. She just wanted to know where she and her son stood. It didn't seem so unreasonable so one afternoon while everyone was at a farewell party for a retiring secretary, I got the keys to Phillip's office off his secretary's desk. His personal file cabinet was unlocked so I just looked until I found a copy of the will. It had been changed and left the bulk of the estate to someone else. This did not seem fair to me. It only took a couple of minutes to photocopy it and return it to the file. No one saw me."

"When she met me later that evening and read the will, she was furious. She said she needed to find those two women before her ex-husband died and talk to them. She wanted them to see how unfair the will was and get them to see reason. I agreed to help her hire private investigators to find them. But I swear to you! I didn't know she would try something like this. I didn't really."

"So Mason, just how much did she pay you to sell out your firm and Mr. Garland?" Jack asked as he got up and took a step toward the lawyer.

Jonathan stepped between them and said, "Hold on, Jack! Let the man finish."

"No, you don't understand, she never paid me anything. She told me she would go right to Phillip and tell him what I had done. I couldn't let him find out. I agreed to help her find Jessica and her mother. They only promised to pay me after they collected their inheritance. I didn't ask any more questions. That is all I know."

Phillip Emery shook his head and said, "What did you suppose they were going to do, Samuel?"

"I don't know. It didn't seem so bad then. I never knew those women. They were strangers to me, and Mrs. Daniels was my client. I felt she needed help. Besides, Thomas Garland was never a friend to me. He only had contempt for whatever I did or said. It was a way of maybe beating him, I guess."

"You just can't imagine how much harm you've done." Jack spoke up. "These people, who are your clients, are planning murder to get this inheritance. How does that set with you now?"

"I never knew that. It wouldn't have occurred to me that they'd go to those extremes. I'm sorry, I didn't know. It hasn't happened though."

"You realize, of course, Samuel, if their plan had succeeded, you could have become an accessory to murder."

"I know it now, Phillip. I realize what harm I've done and I'd like to help to undo it somehow. Their plan hasn't worked yet. The girl is safe enough here. There are ways to get her out of the marriage. After all, we're lawyers."

"Perhaps you're right. It's not hopeless after all. Since you understand the seriousness of your actions, you can stay and help us. Maybe we better talk to Jessica about this. William, please ask her to come down and talk with us."

"All right, I will ask her if she is ready to come down." William said as he left the room.

After the butler had left, the four men sat down and had another cup of tea. No one wanted to speak right away. All were deciding how to tell Jessica ho to get out of her predicament. Jack was sure he would have to get a few punches in on Adrian. Phillip Emery was trying to think of a way to get an annulment. Samuel Mason was hoping he would not get into legal trouble. However, Jonathan was hoping he could be at her side when the moment of confrontation arrived. He only wanted to protect her in any way he possibly could.

All their musings came to an abrupt end when William burst into the room waving an envelope. He cried out, "She's gone. She left a note. What will we do?"

Chapter 27

"Gone? Why would she leave? What does the note say?" Everyone fired the questions at William at the same time.

"I do not know. It is addressed to Jonathan so I thought he should open it."

"Open it, man! What did she say?"

Jonathan opened the note even though his hands trembled. He read the short letter out loud. It said, "Dear Jonathan, Thank you so very much for all your caring and kindness. Even though I have only known you for a few days, I count you as one of my best friends. By the time you read this note, I will probably be back in Harrisonburg. I have to find out the truth for myself. The Bible says that if we have a fault with someone, we should go and make it right. If I have made a mistake in marrying Adrian, I have to make it right. Again, thank you for all your help. Please pray for me. Love, Jessica."

Jack slammed his fist down on the table as he spoke. "Stupid! That's us, just plain stupid! We should have told her about the danger right away. There's no telling what that guy will do to her. If she gets hurt, we're all to blame."

"It's too late now to pass blame. We've got to hurry if we're going to help Jessica." Jonathan said. "If we can decide what to do. What do you think Mr. Emery?"

"Now, Jonathan, you've handled this just fine so far. Give us the tasks to do. The firm's private jet is at the airport, and a phone call can get it ready in a half hour."

"Good thinking! William will show you Mr. Garland's private telephone. You can call the airport from there. Meanwhile, Jack, you get on the other line and call Clyde's Deli. Tell Norma Jean or Clyde what has happened and that Jessica is coming back there alone. See if she has stopped by there. Get one of them to call the police. We'll go straight to Adrian's house as soon as we get there."

"Jonathan, I know I am a lot to blame for what's happened. If you'd let me, I'd like to help. They were never honest with me either."

"Sure, Mr. Mason. We can use all the help we can get. You can pack the tapes in this bag. We may need them soon."

"What can I do, Jonathan?" William was asking him as he turned off the stove.

"All of us can fit into the jet. We had better all go along. Just shut up the house and get ready to go to the airport."

Just then, Mr. Emery returned and reported, "The jet will be ready in about twenty minutes. That is enough time to get to the airport. The pilot is filing emergency flight plans right now."

"I just talked to Clyde." Jack added. "He said Jessica stopped by for a few minutes. She seemed upset but only talked to Norma Jean about how Adrian had been cheating on her and lying to her. When Norma Jean went to get them a cup of coffee, she left the deli but did not say where she was going. They looked for her but she was gone. They are worried."

"She's gone to see Adrian. I'm sure of it. How long ago was she there?"

"He said it was almost two hours ago. He is going to call the police right away."

"Good! Is everyone ready? We've got to hurry!"

All five men ran out the door and jumped into Mr. Mason's car to go to the airport. They hoped they would be in time to prevent anything happening to Jessica. At the airport, the jet was ready and they were able to take off almost immediately.

Jessica drove straight out to the house after she left the deli. As she drove, she rehearsed what she would say to Adrian. Nothing that came to mind made any sense. How could she confront this man who was out to steal and cheat her? She had to think of a way. The only thing to do was to ask him for the truth.

Hoping to arrive at the house quietly, she parked the car at a pull-off on the lane which was beyond the house. She walked down a path in the woods which came out by the back of the house. The fading light of the sunset cast many shadows in the courtyard. The fountain was turned off but gleamed in the last rays of the sun. For a moment she felt like running back to the car and driving away. But she had come this far and she would have to finish it.

Walking around to the front of the house, she stayed close to the walls. The only car parked there was the Simms' van. So Adrian was not at home. She guessed that he must be with his girlfriend at her townhouse. Well, she would wait to go into the house, when he came home. She slipped around to the back of the house and headed for her sanctuary, the gazebo.

From her seat in the gazebo, she could see the house and the driveway. When Adrian came home, she would know. The only light on in the house was in the kitchen. Perhaps Mrs. Simms was fixing supper for her son.

"Her son - her son! What a bunch of liars!" Jessica muttered under her breath. "Can I get any truth out of them?"

Sighing, she sat back and waited. A cooling breeze stirred her hair and jingled the wind chimes. She crossed her arms and wished Adrian would hurry up and come back to the house. She felt cold and so alone.

No sooner had she thought that when she remembered she was never really alone. Jesus, her Savior, was always with her. It gave her comfort to think of her Lord being there. So she bowed her head and spent some time in prayer. An hour passed before her prayer was interrupted as a car pulled into the driveway.

Noiselessly, Jessica crept up to the kitchen window. Since it was a cool evening, the window was open. She took a quick look inside to see who was there. Sitting at the table were Mr. and Mrs. Simms. Their backs were to her but they were the only ones there. Just then, the door opened and Adrian came into the room. She only had a moment to duck as he walked past the window.

Looking back inside, she watched to see what they would do. She felt a little guilty eavesdropping but she had to learn the truth for herself. From her vantage point, it was possible to hear everything they said.

"You look mighty pleased with yourself tonight, Adrian. What has happened?" Mrs. Simms said as she poured a cup of coffee for her son.

"Hey, what can I say? The plan is working perfectly. The old man is dead, and my dear wife is now a very rich woman. Our man, Mason, called me right after the funeral. We're going to have our just due very soon. Oh, how sweet is revenge!"

"As they say, son, don't get too cocky. She might find out just who you are while she is down there. That young lawyer and his detective friend aren't stupid, you know." Mr. Simms added as he sipped his coffee.

"So what if she does find out. It is too late. We are legally married and I'm entitled to any wealth she has. Our vows said for richer or poorer. Well, we've done the poorer so we are now having the richer part. She won't divorce me. You know that."

"True, son, she won't do that. Her religion forbids it. We got her where we want her. She can't do anything about it. How about a bite of supper?"

"No thanks, Mom. Betty fixed up some incredible omelettes for us tonight. Maybe I'd better call my beloved wife and let her know how much I love her and miss her. I'll just beg her to come home because I need her so much. I certainly don't want her to think I don't care about her."

His laughter sent chills up her spine. She wanted to cry or yell at all three of them but she kept silent. Now she must decide whether to run away or stay to learn more of their plans. She had to know more.

For a short time, it was very quiet in the house. She almost slipped away when she heard her husband return and say, "That's odd, no one was at the house. I'll try calling later."

"So when is she coming back? We need to know so we can make our plans."

"When I talk to her, I'll be sure to let her know I need her to come home as soon as possible. I can still do that. She is hopelessly in love with me, you know."

"We will have to wait a little while before staging the accident. It would look suspicious her dying so soon after inheriting a lot of money."

"No way, Mom! No one will think that. The accident will look so real that they will only think how tragic it is that she didn't get to enjoy her wealth. I can put on quite a show of being sorrowful."

"All right, you've convinced me, Adrian. Just how do you propose to do it?"

"I was trying to decide between a car accident or maybe a fall in the house. I favor the car, myself. Either way, she'll be just as dead and I'll be a very rich widower."

Jessica slapped her hand across her mouth to suppress the scream which rose in her throat. This was even worse than she imagined. Why had not they told her about this? Did they know about this part of the plan? Now she realized just how dangerous her situation had become. She had to get back into town and let her friends help her.

It had become quiet in the house. She looked into the window just as she heard a step behind her. Then everything went dark.

Chapter 28

Voices sounded around her as though she was lying in a tunnel. She knew that someone was talking but she was not able to understand any words. Her head hurt and her eyes refused to focus. What happened? How could she have been so foolish?

As her eyes began to focus on the room, she realized she was on a couch in the living room. Across the room, Mr. and Mrs. Simms were sitting and talking. She decided to pretend to still be unconscious. Perhaps that way she could stall for time and learn their plans. Her only hope would be that her friends would find her in time.

"So she's still out." Adrian said as he entered the room. "You hit her too hard, Dad. No matter, it will still fit into our plans."

"Adrian, is this necessary? I mean, couldn't we do this legally? We could get your mother's lawyer, Mason, to do this for us."

"No, Dad, it won't work. She'll not divorce me. Even if she did we'd only get a little of the estate. I want it all. Are you still in this, Mother?"

"Of course, I am. We'd better do it quickly. She knows too much already. Every minute we delay gives her friends time to find us."

"Maybe, Nora, they don't know she's here?"

"Edward, they will figure it out. Where else would she go but to see her husband? We have very little time."

"You're right. We certainly don't know how much they've guessed about our plan. By now, they know about me being the old man's son. If they got that much, it won't be difficult to figure out who you two are."

"Let's get it over with. I don't like it but it was part of the plan. What do you want me to do?"

"Her car is parked down the lane in that small clearing. Bring it here and you can help me get her into it. Mother and I will take it the top on the other side of the mountain. Plenty of people have taken those curves too fast. She'll just be one more. We should be back in half an hour. Then I'll wait for the state police to bring me the sad news."

"But wait! What could be the reason for her running off the road? It's a clear night and the roads are dry."

"Not to worry. We just need to give her a stiff drink, enough to make the police believe she was drunk. That would do it."

"No, Adrian, that won't do. Everyone knows she doesn't drink alcohol in any form. They'll suspect something."

"Another thing, son. What will be the reason she was driving up there anyway? It is a little bit out of the way."

"We'll just say she drove up there so she'd have a quiet place to think or something. There is a nice view from up there."

"Let me think a moment. We need to come up with a reason for her losing control of the car. What..."

"Hey, wait a minute." Adrian said as he jumped up. "Go get the car, Dad! When you come back in, bring her purse with you. She didn't have it with her so it must be in the car."

Jessica heard the older man leave the house. She was getting quite nervous and could feel her heart racing. Now she was not sure how long she could remain still while they plotted to kill her. She wanted to jump and attempt to run out the door and into the woods. However, she knew she would not get far before they caught her and dragged her back. Again she decided to stay quiet.

Soon Edward came back and handed her purse to Adrian. "Here it is, Adrian. How is it going to help us?"

"I've found it, Mother. She's always taking this sinus medicine. If I haven't missed the point, this type of medication tends to make her drowsy. All we need to do is wake her up and get a few of these down her throat. When they do an autopsy, they'll find all these drugs in her blood. They'll assume she took some and then went out. While driving on the mountain, she passed out and drove off the road and over the cliff. Clever?"

"Not just clever. Brilliant is more like it. Well, don't stand there, Edward, help us with her."

Rough hands grabbed at her as she tried to squirm out of their grasp. Adrian slapped her as he shouted, "Hey, she's awake. I bet she has been faking being out all along. Let's get her into the kitchen."

Calling out for help was useless as they were so far away from other houses. They dragged her into the kitchen. She put up a vain struggle as they opened her mouth and pushed tablets into it. She nearly choked but they prevailed as she was forced to swallow. Their only kindness was to give her two sips of water before they tied and gagged her. The two men picked her up and dumped her into the back floor of her car.

Her last thoughts were a prayer. "Please, dear Lord, help me. Bring my friends to help me." As she heard the engine start up, she blacked out.

At the airport, the jet had only just stopped when several police cars pulled up to the runway. Jonathan and the others hurried off the plane. Stepping out of one of the cars were Clyde and Norma Jean.

"Jonathan, over here! There's not a minute to lose!" Clyde shouted.

"Hey, Clyde. How did you get all these police?"

"It took some fast talking, believe you me. Get in and I'll tell you on the way."

Jonathan and the others jumped into the cars. Sirens blared as they raced out into the night.

"Ok, Clyde. Tell all! We only expected to see you and Norma Jean."

"It seems like this guy, Adrian, and his girlfriend had been running some financial scams. The police were only waiting to get enough evidence to go after them."

"This afternoon, they had decided it was time to move in on the operation. They nabbed the girl first at her townhouse. She had been talking to them for a couple of hours when I called. They realized the danger and sent a squad car to his house. We're heading there now. Let's hope we're in time."

No one spoke as they raced through the night to find Jessica. Jonathan desperately prayed that they would be in time.

Just as they went past the mall, a radio call came in. Jonathan listened as well as he could but it was hard to make sense of what they were saying over the noise of the sirens. The officer in the passenger side of the car talked to the dispatcher for a few minutes.

As soon as he signed off, he turned back to Jonathan and said, "Our men at the house just radioed us. Seems the stepfather, a Mr. Simms, was the only person there. He talked pretty freely when he learned it was all up. His wife and Daniels took the girl, Jessica, up to the top of an old mountain road. A lot of accidents happen there because of all the curves on the road. Their intentions are to push the car down the road with the girl in it. They've got about a ten minute start on us. But on this side of the mountain, the road is fairly straight and we can make good time. If we're lucky we can almost beat them to the top."

"Why didn't Adrian go that way also? It is a much shorter distance from his house."

"That's true. However, on this side of the mountain, the road is blocked by a locked gate. I've told the dispatcher to call the caretaker who lives near the gate to meet us there and unlock it for us."

"Good job, Officer!"

Norma Jean spoke up. "Please hurry, officer. That gal is my best friend. If he hurts her, he'll have me to deal with."

"He'll have the whole police force to deal with. We're doing all we can."

"I sure hope you are praying, Jonathan, because only God can save her now. We need a real miracle to slow them down."

"Right, Norma Jean. God can work a miracle. Will you pray with us Clyde?"

"I've never been much on praying all my life. But I'm smart enough to know when to ask for help from someone stronger than me. Yeah, count me in."

The three in the back seat bowed their heads and joined hands. Each asked God for a miracle to reach down and delay the car with Jessica in it. That was their only hope now.

Soon they were passing through the gate and climbing up the mountain. Abruptly, the cars cut off the sirens. The sudden quiet was unnerving at first as they had gotten used to all the noise. They seemed to creep up the mountain. When they reached the summit, it was dark and there were no other cars there. The three police cars pulled to the side and turned off all their lights. Quietly, some of the policemen and Jack got out and went into the bushes on both sides of the road.

One officer remained in the car. "I think we have somehow got here first. My men will carefully approach the car as soon as they get out. They'll need to turn the car around. That wide spot there is the only place to do it coming up that side of the mountain. Also they'll need to get out in order to push the car. We can grab them then. I don't know how we got here first but we did. Maybe your prayers worked. Shh! There are lights coming."

Now they could see it also. Car lights were snaking their way up the mountain. Jonathan could only hope that the police cars were well hidden around the curve in the road. The officers in the bushes were well hidden and he did not know where they were. He knew they only had a few moments and he prayed even more.

As the first car pulled into the wide spot, it skidded to a halt. With the lights still on, he could see a rather large woman get out and open the rear passenger door. At that point, two of the police jumped out of the bushes and grabbed her around the waist. At that moment, a second car with Adrian turned the last curve. He could plainly see what was going on and he spun his car around in the circle. Several officers tried to block his way but he was too fast for them. He then sped off down the mountain. Two of the policemen ran back to their car and followed him at a slower speed.

Jonathan jumped out and ran over to the car which was now surrounded by police officers. Mrs. Simms had given up struggling and was all ready handcuffed and being led to a police car. Sitting on the ground and being untied was Jessica with Norma Jean holding on to her friend. Clyde was standing over both of them. The young woman groaned and opened her eyes. For a moment, she looked like she was dead. Now he was so relieved and happy to see she was just fine.

Norma Jean was crying and said, "Honey, are you okay? It's Norma Jean and Clyde. Jonathan is right here, too. Please speak to us."

"Norma Jean? What happened? Where are we? The last I remember is those people putting me in this car?"

Jonathan spoke up, "Don't worry any. We stopped them from hurting you. The police have your mother-in-law and father-in-law in custody so they can't hurt you now."

"Thank God, you're here Jonathan. I was praying God would get you here in time. But where's Adrian? He was in another car right behind us."

"He took off down the mountain but the police are right behind him. He won't get away. They blocked the entrance to the road at the bottom of the mountain. He's as good as caught."

Just as he said that, an explosion echoed across the glens in the mountain. Before the last echo died, they all knew what had happened to Adrian. Mrs. Simms screamed and fainted in the police car. Jessica grabbed Jonathan and cried on his chest. He held on to her and stroked her head. "It's going to be all right, darling Jessica. I'm here to take care of you. It's all over now. You're safe and that's all that matters to me. . .I love you, Jessica."

Chapter 29

Three days later, Jessica sat in a bright hospital room. All around her were flowers and balloons, giving the room the appearance of a floral shop. She sighed and smiled at all the tokens of love and friendship. She had not known she had so many friends.

She looked at each of the arrangements and remembered who had sent it to her. Mr. Mason, her uncle's partner, had sent a dozen white roses with a long note asking her forgiveness for his part in the plot against her. Of course, she forgave him. There were flowers from Norma Jean, Clyde and the other waitresses at the deli. William had sent some lovely pink carnations. The single yellow rose was from Jack. But her favorite was the red and white roses from Jonathan. She just had to smile whenever she thought about him who had been so sweet and loving to her.

Then she thought back to the two previous days and wondered how she had survived them. That night when she almost lost her life was a nightmare which she could not forget. She was still bewildered at how they had wanted to kill her.

Now the Simms, or really the Daniels, had lost more than their money or their freedom. They had lost their only son in a horrible way. She almost felt sorry for them, but it might take time to fully forgive them. Her friends had finally told her that Adrian's car had run off the road and crashed into a deep ravine. He had been killed instantly when the car burst into flame and exploded. The fate he had planned for her had become his. The funeral was set for that afternoon, but she was glad she would not be able to attend. That chapter of her life was closed.

So captivated was she by her thoughts that she did not hear a knock on her door. When she failed to respond, Jonathan came inside. Seeing her sitting up in the hospital bed, he smiled and said, "Earth to Jessica, come in, Jessica."

She looked up to see him. He looked so fresh and good in his jeans and tee shirt. His smile was just what she wanted to see. "Jonathan, I was hoping you'd come soon. I guess I was daydreaming when you knocked. Please, sit down. You can stay awhile, can't you?"

"I sure can't refuse your kind invitation. As for the length of my stay, you tell me when to go and I'll go. Otherwise, I can stay a long time. I brought you some fruit but I can't see where to put it with all these flowers. Here's a place. Would you like some of it?"

"No, thanks. What I would like is some answers to a lot of questions. I think I can take all the truth now."

"Ask your questions. I'll do my best to answer them."

"First of all, I just don't understand about how Adrian could have so totally deceived me. How did he find out who I was? How did he make me believe he had a lot of money? I'm so confused about it all."

"As you know, Mr. Mason in the law firm was his mother's attorney. He gave them a copy of the will. They also hired a private investigator to look for you just as your uncle did. There was always someone one step ahead of us. I'm sorry they found you first."

"Your second question had me puzzled for quite a while. This morning before he left for North Carolina, Jack gave me a copy of the police questioning of Mr. and Mrs. Daniels, a.k.a. the Simms'. They pretty much told the whole story."

"How did Jack get that?"

"He has a way of getting things done. Anyhow, I'll give you the highlights of what they revealed. If you'd like to read it, I'll leave a copy with you. Their whole plan was to convince you of his wealth. They used their savings and her alimony money to buy the clothes and fancy gifts. Everything else, the cars and the house were leased for six months. If Mr. Garland had held on to life much longer they were in trouble. They were behind in all their payments."

"But how did he possibly afford all those trips to other countries? He sent me letters from so many places."

"Really, it was easy because he never left town. He had friends who were living in other countries. They were also into his financial planning schemes. When he told you he was going to South Africa, he would send a letter to you to a friend in Johannesburg. The friend would take the letter out, attach postage and mail it back to you. There it is, he had been to South Africa."

"Why did those people do that for him? It's so deceitful."

"Some of them were his accomplices in the financial scam he was running. Some of them only seem to be friends. He told them he was playing a joke on his girlfriend. It sounded harmless enough."

"True, that was pretty slick. What about our trip to Hawaii? How did he afford it?"

"Now, here was a stroke only of luck for them. His parents had actually won a trip for two to Hawaii. They agreed to let Adrian take you with the hope of taking a trip after they got the inheritance."

"What about the woman whom Adrian was dating? How did she figure into the scheme? What will happen to her now? In a way, I feel sorry for her. Adrian used her, too."

"She really needs our prayers. When they told her Adrian was dead, she broke down. Right now she is in this hospital under a careful watch to make sure she doesn't kill herself. She has been silent since that night and will not answer any questions. Her part was she loved a man who only used her for his own purposes. She says she was not aware that Adrian's business dealings which he ran out of her townhouse were illegal."

"They had been living together for a couple of years before the Daniels' hatched their plot. She just would have overlooked anything bad in his life or done anything for him. Whenever Adrian was supposed to be out of town or at work, he kept out of sight at her place. He had her completely in his control. She may still face some charges regarding the financial scam."

"Oh, no, that is awful! I guess I can sympathize with her about being fooled by Adrian. He was good at it." She paused for a moment and continued, "You may think this very strange but I'd like to see her and help her in any way I can. What's the use of having all this money if I can't use it to help others?"

"Have you forgiven her?"

"Yes, I have. She, of course, hasn't asked me to forgive her but I know I can. The Lord said we were to love and forgive those who have wronged us. He, Himself, set the example for us. In fact, I believe I can forgive them all. Life is too short to hold on to resentments and be unforgiving."

"You've changed, Jessica."

"No, not really. God brought me back to Him for His own purpose and plan. He touched my heart which was hard and cold and made it alive and warm again. I just hope I can see the good that He planned to come out of this."

"Don't you see it? It's all ready begun. Your uncle is in Heaven right now on account of your testimony and witness. As a result of his conversion and witness to William, he has been saved. Even Jack is investigating Christ's claims in his own way. I've caught him regarding the Gideon Bibles a number of times in motel rooms. I plan to give him a Bible the next time I see him. Clyde has decided to go to church with Norma Jean and her family. He'll hear more of the Gospel there. It wouldn't surprise me to hear of his conversion soon."

"Praise the Lord, Jonathan. Maybe I can get a chance to witness to Adrian's parents and Betty. It might make a difference if I tell them I forgive them. Then they will understand God's forgiveness much better."

"There is one question I have for you, Jessica. That night when we rescued you, we were all praying for God to delay your car long enough so we would reach the top of the mountain first. What happened?"

"I'm not really sure because I was lying on the back floor board of the rented car which she was driving. My mind was not clear because of the drugs I had been given. I do remember her slamming on the brakes and swearing about a train. She got out of the car for a few minutes. I heard her talking to Adrian who said a tree had fallen on the tracks. The train could not move until the tree was removed and it was blocking the road. We were only stopped for a little while, maybe only a few minutes."

"Wow! It may have been only a few minutes but it was sure an answer to prayer. What a miracle! God knocked a tree down to stop a train to delay the cars. Just wait until I tell the others."

Bending over her, he kissed her on the cheek. She grasped his hand and said, "One last question, Jonathan. That night when I was crying on your shoulder, I heard or thought I heard you say something like, 'I love you, Jessica.' Did you...mean that?"

Jonathan took both her hands in his and whispered, "Yes, I did and I meant it. I've been in love with you for a while now. I can only hope maybe one day, you'd..."

"Jonathan, I'm so confused and afraid of these feelings. Can you give us a little time? Will you be here?"

Taking her into his arms, he kissed her gently. They held on to each other as if they never wanted to let go. "You can be sure of one thing. I'll be here. There is plenty of time now."

Printed in the United States
58706LVS00004B/52-102